Volume Eight

Airship 27 Productions

Sinbad the New Voyages Volume 8

"The Tournament Fantastic" © 2025 Erik Franklin
"Nymph Mania" © 2025 Carson Demmans
"The Old Man of the Sea" © 2025 Terry Wjesuriya
"The Hittite Sword God" © 2025 J. Walt Layne

Published by Airship 27 Productions
www.airship27.com
www.airship27hangar.com

Interior illustrations © 2025 Gary Kato
Cover illustration © 2025 Michael Youngblood

Editor: Ron Fortier
Associate Editor: Jaime Ramos
Marketing and Promotions Manager: Michael Vance
Art Director/Designer: Rob Davis

ISBN: 978-1-953589-96-5

Printed in the United States of America

10 9 8 7 6 5 4 3 2 1

## Volume Eight Contents

# THE TOURNAMENT FANTASTIC

## by Erik Franklin

**W**hat promised to be a relaxing, blissful shore leave turned into a nightmare as soon as the crew of the Blue Nymph arrived at the dock. Sinbad stepped off of his ship and onto the wet wooden planks. His athletic physique, finely trimmed Van Dyke beard, brown skin and piercing blue eyes caught the eye of every woman near him. Sinbad paid no attention to them, for he found himself gazing at the Blue Nymph. He smiled at his pride and joy, admiring the strong, formidable vessel. Her main sail caught the sunlight, bathing Sinbad in an indigo hue. Sinbad turned and looked at the vast city before him, making a mental list of tasks he needed to accomplish in order to have the Blue Nymph seaworthy again and his crew appropriately provided for. All of this was brushed aside by the sudden appearance of a man rushing towards Sinbad. He wore the uniform of one of the Sultan's servants and carried a note in his hand.

"Are you Sinbad El Ari, Captain of the Blue Nymph?" the servant asked with a note of urgency in his voice.

"Yes, and who may you be?" Sinbad inquired, noticing the worried expression on the man's face.

"Please, read this note and follow me, Sinbad!" the servant said as he caught his breath. Sinbad hurriedly opened the note and read:

*Sinbad, the Sultan Nesuah is gravely ill and desires to see you. Meet me in my chambers after you have seen him. - Krassa*

Though Sinbad had been to the Sultan's palace many times, he did not recognize the name Krassa. The thought of his ailing friend was foremost in his mind. Sinbad saw his first mate, Omar, giving orders to the crew and called out to him.

"Omar!"

His first mate quickly turned to face him, his husky frame tensed, ready to do whatever Sinbad ordered. "Yes, Captain? We're getting the cargo ready that you..."

"Yes, yes!" Sinbad said dismissively, waving away Omar's speech. "Omar, you are captain while I am away. I need to see the Sultan!"

And with that, Sinbad sprinted off to the Sultan's palace with the servant in tow.

Sinbad walked briskly into the large, opulent bedroom of Nesuah. Crossing the room, which was covered with an ornately patterned Persian rug, the sailor respectfully approached the solid gold bed frame and looked upon a frail, older man whom he regarded as a surrogate father. Sinbad began to speak, but the words were stuck in his throat. It had been many moons since Sinbad had laid eyes upon the old man, but he had remembered him as being vital, robust, a man who lived life to the fullest. Now, the sound of Nesuah's cough felt like a dagger being plunged into Sinbad's heart.

Before Sinbad became the legendary adventurer, sailor, and captain of the Blue Nymph... he was the spoiled son of a Nubian prince and Moorish princess. Sinbad had squandered his family's fortune by indulging himself excessively in all manner of materialistic pleasures.

Sinbad's poor choices had alienated him from any person of good standing, so he was forced to buy the majority of his "friendships." When his wealth had been depleted, his friends moved on, abandoning him like vultures do after picking a corpse clean. The only man who still believed in Sinbad was Nesuah. Though he was displeased by the young man's actions, Nesuah was persistent in his conviction that Sinbad would realize his folly and become a man of honor.

Nesuah's subjects considered him a wise ruler, and he was fond of telling all who doubted his word, "You will see, I am an old soul who knows much, and I will be right in the end. Sinbad is destined for great things... this I know!" He said this with a smile, and when he eventually was proven correct, Nesuah was graceful when accepting their apology. Every time that Sinbad was in port, he made the time to see his old friend. The Sultan sat back, eagerly listening to the sailor regale him with tales of his adventures.

All of that seemed like a distant memory to Sinbad now, as he looked into the once sparkling eyes of the dying Sultan.

"Sinbad... tell me of your adventures." Nesuah said between his deep and painful coughs. This was the Sultan's customary greeting to his friend, but Sinbad was in no mood for storytelling.

"My friend, is there anything I can do for you? I will go to the ends of the earth to help you!" Sinbad pledged, his eyes blazing with conviction.

Nesuah made a great effort and placed his cold, bony hand on Sinbad's taut, muscular outstretched hand. "There is nothing that can be done for me...

Sinbad... It happened so suddenly... I cannot remember.... But I am being kept quite comfortable... Now, please, one of your stories..."

Sinbad was disturbed at seeing the Sultan in this state, but thought questioning Nesuah would upset the ailing man. He thought of the note that Krassa had sent, and vowed to discover what had caused this calamity to befall his friend. In the meantime, Sinbad related the tale of his most recent adventure, doing his best to summon the same gusto and bravado he had used in relating his other voyages. The Sultan listened with wrapped attention, flashing the same boyish smile he always did when he was captivated by one of Sinbad's adventures.

"Thank you, Sinbad." Nesuah said once the sailor finished his narrative. "... that was your most thrilling one yet." He always said this to Sinbad once his stories were finished, and he meant it each and every time.

"I look forward to telling you many more, my friend." Sinbad said, encouraging the dying Sultan to rally his strength. "I will see you soon."

"I hope so... Sinbad..." Nesuah said between coughs as Sinbad parted company with him. He thought back to the note he received from the servant, and then he decided to begin his investigation into the Sultan's mysterious illness by speaking with this Krassa.

Not knowing where to begin his search, Sinbad approached the first palace guard he saw and showed him the letter.

"Excuse me, I am attempting to find this man, Krassa. Do you know if he is here?" Sinbad asked. The guard looked at the letter and scrunched up his face, as if he had just smelled something foul.

"Yes, Krassa, is here," the guard said, "but I would not trust him."

"Why not?" Sinbad asked, beginning to feel wary. Whoever this Krassa was, Sinbad thought it best to be on his guard.

"He is an alchemist, and has promised to heal the Sultan. He has been here for three months, but the Sultan is still a weak man." The guard said bitterly, looking down an elaborately decorated marble hallway. Sinbad assumed that this was where he could find the alchemist.

"The Sultan has been sick for three months!" Sinbad exclaimed. "What happened?"

"No one knows. Many whisper that his enemies have poisoned him, though, as I said, no one knows for sure." The guard said, then he pointed with his spear, "You can find the alchemist at the end of the hall... follow the smell."

Sinbad thanked the guard and wandered down the hall. Halfway to the alchemist's chambers, Sinbad suddenly understood what the guard was referring to. A horrendous odor reached Sinbad's nostrils, and he quickly plugged his nose as he proceeded.

Soon, Sinbad came to a newly installed iron door, where the odor was much worse, and he knocked. "Enter!" an impatient voice bellowed from within, and Sinbad obeyed.

Inside, Sinbad was met by a balding man in a long, elegant, flowing robe. His white beard came to a pointed tip under his chin while his white, bushy eyebrows threatened to engulf his eyes. The man, whom Sinbad took to be Krassa, was busy mixing and stirring a potion, pulling ingredients from the numerous chemical stained shelves that lined the room. He glanced up at Sinbad with an expectant look in his eye.

"Are you Sinbad El Ari?" Krassa asked, with an edge to his voice that suggested great trouble if he was not.

"Yes, and you are Krassa, I assume? I have your letter..." Sinbad said, producing the document, but Krassa dismissed it.

"Good, good. You have not come a moment too soon, Sinbad!" Krassa said as he sprinkled in some herbs that were lying on a nearby bench in a bubbling cauldron. As he resumed his work, Krassa became seemingly oblivious to Sinbad's presence, absorbed in perfecting his brew.

"I understand that the Sultan has been poisoned..." Sinbad said, attempting to begin his investigation.

"Poisoned! Bah! That is what I told those simpleton guards and royal advisers! Poisoned indeed!" Krassa stepped away from the now-simmering concoction and leaned in close to Sinbad. Keeping his voice low, the old alchemist whispered, "The Sultan has been cursed by dark magic."

"Dark magic?" Sinbad repeated, aghast.

Krassa nodded grimly, "Yes, the darkest kind of magic. I have been able to delay the magic's ill effects, but if nothing changes over the course of this month, the Sultan will die."

"What have you done for Nesuah? Is there a medicine or...?" Sinbad said, but the alchemist's shaking head cut his sentence short.

"I am afraid not, Sinbad. I have been able to relieve his pain and ease his suffering, but alas, the magic is too powerful. There is but one last desperate course of action. Let me preface my plan by saying..."

"Just tell me, what is your plan? I will do anything to save Nesuah's life!" Sinbad pleaded.

Krassa walked away from Sinbad and back to his potion. As he stirred and added various ingredients to the odorous liquid, he spoke quickly. "There is a special crystal that has the ability to heal any ailment, even if one is on the verge of death."

"Where is it? I will recover it and bring it to the Sultan!" Sinbad insisted, his blue eyes burning with determination.

"That is the challenging part..." Krassa said, his voice descending to a downcast tone.

"I have been on many voyages, Krassa. There is no place on earth that my crew and I cannot find!" Sinbad said assuredly.

"I know that you are a great sailor and captain, but it is your skills as a warrior that might save the Sultan. You see, the crystal is in the possession of a dark and dangerous man. He has created what he calls: The Tournament Fantastic. The crystal is to be rewarded to the champion of the tournament," Krassa explained.

"I have won fighting tournaments before, my crew and I are ready for any challenge!" Sinbad said confidently.

"I assure you that you have never been in a tournament such as this... but before we continue... I need you to drink this potion that I have been brewing." Krassa said, and to Sinbad's chagrin, it was the same foul potion that he was laboring on for the duration of the conversation.

"Why? How will this help?" Sinbad asked, dubious and wary of the merits of Krassa's potion and the alchemist himself.

"This potion I am brewing can only be consumed once. If taken more than once, then the drinker's life is forfeited. Once consumed, this potion reveals to you what you desire most in the world." Krassa explained.

"It sounds incredible, but why do I have to drink this?"

Krassa replied, "*I* needed to drink it in order to see the crystal in the Tournament Fantastic. Then my vision faded before it could reveal the location of the island battleground. When you drink it, *you* will know where to sail to find the Tournament Fantastic!" Krassa exclaimed, bringing the clear vial of bubbling green liquid over to Sinbad. "Concentrate on the journey! Think: Where do I sail to find the Tournament Fantastic?"

"And once I find the way... your plan is to have me win the tournament and claim the crystal as the prize?" Sinbad said, again dubious about the feasibility of this scheme. "You make it sound too simple, alchemist."

"I can only tell you what my vision revealed. Now, Sinbad, do you want to save the Sultan's life or not?" Krassa demanded.

Taking the vial from the alchemist's hand, Sinbad, mustering his courage and suppressing his urge to vomit, downed the foul, rancid potion in one miserable gulp.

"This tastes even worse than it smells!" Sinbad yelled as soon as he was able.

"Concentrate, Sinbad! Close your eyes and think of your voyage to the tournament!" Krassa urged.

Doing as he was told, Sinbad closed his eyes, and suddenly he saw visions as if a tapestry had come to life in front of him! He saw his ship, the Blue

Nymph, making its way from the harbor, and setting sail to an island that he had not previously encountered. Once there he saw a towering, monolithic stone platform built on the edge of a cliff. As his vision faded, he saw himself ascending the stairs alone. His vision was replaced by blackness once more. He opened his eyes to find Krassa looking at him expectantly.

"What did you see?" Krassa asked.

Sinbad told the old alchemist what he had witnessed, to which Krassa replied, "Then I think you know what you must do, Sinbad. I wish you the best of luck."

Sinbad nodded. He left the palace and headed for the docks. True, his crew would grumbled at their shore leave being cut short after only a few hours, but the Sultan's life was in his hands.

"What do you mean *alone!*" Ralf Gunarson yelled as he slammed his fist down on the table. Sinbad had found some of his crew in a tavern near the port, and relayed the story to them, and his intention to travel alone.

"I stand by our Captain's decision. I do not even know the Sultan or have any interest in this tournament in the first place. Why shouldn't our brave Captain venture forth alone?" Henri Delacrois said as he savored every bite of his apple.

Ralf looked at Henri with contempt. The two could not have been more opposite. Ralf was a gigantic, gruff Viking, and Henri was a handsome, charming archer from Gaul. Both served Sinbad loyally, though their reasons for embarking on these quests were quite different. Ralf wanted the danger, Henri wanted the reward. Sinbad knew that he could rely on them, but also knew that telling them of his quest to aid the Sultan would not be easy.

"Do you mean to say there is a tournament, and you are not using your strongest fighter! Can you explain the wisdom of that decision, Captain!" Ralf yelled while grasping his flagon of wine so tightly that Sinbad feared the metal would bend.

"As I have said, my vision showed me going alone, so I have decided to follow my own prophecy." Sinbad said plainly.

"There you have it. I will follow your orders to the letter, Captain." Henri said, delighted that he was out of danger.

"I am relying on you two to round up the others while I make preparations for us to sail." Sinbad said, before turning back to them with a look of concern on his face. "That will not take long, will it?"

"Tishimi wanted to remain on deck, practicing with that magic sword of hers," Henri said, his eyes narrowing as he tried to remember the locations of the rest. "Haroun, Omar, and Rafi are restocking the ship while we are in port, and William is with us, he went to fetch us something to eat."

Sinbad nodded and headed back to the Blue Nymph. Henri looked over to see Ralf looking at him with a dark expression on his face.

"You disgust me." Ralf said, and by the sound of his voice, the wine was beginning to dull his mind.

"Come now, Ralf, we need to get the others back on the boat, just like the Captain ordered." Henri said.

"Why is it that you are *so* afraid to die, Henri?" Ralf asked, one part angry, one part curious, and the other part drunk.

"Perhaps no one has explained the benefits of dying to me," Henri said as he made his way to William.

"If you die fighting well... you go to Valhalla! Where you are in the company of the finest warriors... such as myself," Ralf offered.

"I will spend my entire afterlife in the company of men like you?" Henri asked.

"Yah!"

"That is a good reason to fear death," Henri said.

The journey was uneventful, though Sinbad felt his tension grow as they sailed closer to the island in his vision. Lost in his thoughts, Sinbad was startled when Haroun, the ship's lookout, cupped his hands to his mouth and called out:

"Land ho! Land ho!"

Just as Sinbad had seen in his vision, a towering monolith stood at the edge of the cliff, with a spiral staircase wrapped around the structure like a giant, stone anaconda. His crew stood before him, assembled and anxious. Though resentful of being left behind, Ralf looked on at Sinbad with pride, respecting the courage of his leader. Henri, though attempting to show his usual bravado, looked downcast. Tishimi Osara, the female samurai, looked nervously at Sinbad. Though she was a woman of few words, her eyes spoke volumes. She was unhappy at seeing Sinbad leave, and wished she could accompany him. Not for the glory of battle, but to ensure his survival. Omar, Haroun, and Rafi watched their Captain stoically, though in their hearts they were wishing him to stay. It was the battle-scarred Scottish warrior, William Bryne, who spoke.

"We wish you the best, Sinbad, and the moment you signal, we will be there." He said, placing a hand on Sinbad's shoulder. Sinbad nodded with a sigh.

Sinbad rowed a small boat to the island. It was at least an hour's worth of walking and climbing to go from the beach to the base of the monolith. Sinbad craned his head backwards and saw that there was a platform located at the top of the monolith, and he swore that he could see a figure looking down upon him. It was a hazy, black silhouette with the blazing sun surrounding its large form. Sinbad cupped his hands to his mouth and called out.

"Hello, friend!" Sinbad ventured, but he saw the mysterious figure walk away from the edge of the platform. After a few moments, it was obvious that the stranger was not going to come down from his perch, so Sinbad was forced to ascend.

Sinbad began to sprint up the stairs, remembering that the Sultan's life was in his hands. However, after a few minutes of running, Sinbad began to feel his muscles tighten and his resolve weaken. He looked up to discover that, despite all of his effort, he still had a long way to go. He glanced at his ship, the Blue Nymph, floating on the calm, blue sea in the distance. He remembered that his vision showed him climbing the structure by himself, and though he dared not deviate from this prophecy, Sinbad wished that his crew would have accompanied him. Conserving his strength, Sinbad walked up the steps, reliving the memories of the dying Sultan to give him courage.

To Sinbad's aching legs and feet, it felt like hours before he reached the top of the platform. When he finally reached it, he saw a tall figure wearing leather gloves, raven black robes, and a dark headwrap. The only bit of flesh that was visible was a narrow slit in the headwrap, and the man's eyes appeared to be black. Though the mysterious figure's arms were crossed, Sinbad noticed that the gloved hands twitched, as the figure's left hand slowly moved towards the sword at his side.

Catching his breath, Sinbad spoke to the figure, "Why did you not answer when I called for you?"

"You addressed me as 'friend.' We are not friends, Sinbad," the figure stated bluntly. Sinbad felt flustered and surprised by the man's directness and that he knew his name. Sinbad watched the man crook his head curiously, as if studying him.

"How did you know my name?" Sinbad asked in wonder. The mysterious fellow offered no reply, so Sinbad cleared his throat and continued.

"I am here to enter the Tournament Fantastic. I only know that I am supposed to be here in order to continue on my voyage.... somehow. Can you help me?" Sinbad ventured, not feeling particularly optimistic that the man would respond favorably.

"Yes, I can take you to the Tournament Fantastic. I am the Gatekeeper for the combatants," the black clad greeter said, his body visibly relaxing. Sinbad was pleased by the response, and allowed himself to feel hopeful once again.

"Well... Gatekeeper, what must I do in order to enter the Tournament Fantastic?" Sinbad inquired.

"Survive," the Gatekeeper said simply.

Sinbad was momentarily confused, though the Gatekeeper's meaning became instantly clear. The black figure unsheathed his sword and began slashing furiously at Sinbad! Sinbad's legs were tired and weary, and it was all that the sailor could do to keep away from the Gatekeeper's deadly blade! Rolling, dodging, and tumbling, Sinbad managed to create enough distance between them in order to unsheathe his own curved sword.

The Gatekeeper stopped his assault as the two circled each other, now equals on the battlefield. Sinbad studied his opponent silently, though the Gatekeeper spoke his thoughts out loud.

"You possess great agility... you are clever... not impulsive... Now we will see how you fight!" The Gatekeeper said as he charged at Sinbad.

Sinbad, now ready for the Gatekeeper's assault, was prepared to defend himself. Their blades clashed with tremendous force, and Sinbad was surprised at the Gatekeeper's strength! If Sinbad had not held onto his sword as firmly as he did, the weapon would have flown from his hand over the cliff and into the ocean below.

Sinbad felt that the Gatekeeper's strength outmatched his, and though he was able to evade the Gatekeeper's strikes, the legendary sailor was unsure of how to defeat this foe. He parried each of the Gatekeeper's attacks, yet Sinbad was unable to see an opening to strike back. Sinbad was already growing weary, and he knew that the Gatekeeper could sense this.

"You are tired... your endurance is reaching its limit... your strength is waning... if you are unable to defeat me, you will die... along with your dream of entering the Tournament Fantastic," the powerful guard taunted.

Sinbad was desperate, the Sultan's life rested in his hands, and he was not about to let an old friend down. He had a plan, the only thing he could think of, and he risked losing everything if he failed.

During the battle, Sinbad had managed to get the Gatekeeper positioned near the edge of the platform, and he hurled his sword with all of his might at the Gatekeeper's head. The Gatekeeper parried the blade, sending Sinbad's sword plummeting into the ocean below... but Sinbad had anticipated this. While the Gatekeeper parried, he had left himself vulnerable. Sinbad raced towards the dark figure and leapt at him with a flying kick!

Sinbad felt his foot connect against a hard, well-muscled chest and watched as the Gatekeeper plummeted from the platform and fell to the ocean below. Sinbad collapsed onto the platform, exhausted. He was breathing hard, his

"SURVIVE," THE GATEKEEPER SAID SIMPLY.

muscles aching and drenched in sweat. Still, he could not help but smile... He had not only survived, but he had won! Surely, this was a good omen of things to come!

Rest, however, was not in store for Sinbad. He suddenly saw the Gatekeeper fly up from out of the ocean and hover over him. To Sinbad's amazement, the sentinel had sprouted titanic, raven-like wings! The Gatekeeper removed his headwrap, and Sinbad saw that he was not fighting a man, but a gigantic, humanoid raven!

"You fight well, Sinbad El Ari. Few have defeated me, and this has earned you a favorable position in the tournament. I will take you there presently."

Before Sinbad could say anything, the Gatekeeper's boots burst open to reveal the black, taloned feet of a raven. The Gatekeeper rapidly swooped down and Sinbad felt the raven-man's taloned toes close around his arms and whisk him off of the platform.

The birdman flew swiftly over the land with Sinbad in his clutches, as the now helpless adventurer watched the ground rush underneath them. He saw the Blue Nymph become a speck on the ocean and a new structure came into view ahead of them. Sinbad's jaw dropped as he saw the incredible sight of Lord Yar's Coliseum.

What was once a mountaintop had become a gigantic, stone arena. Round in design, the facade was decorated with massive stone statues of mythological creatures. Sinbad could discern a crowd of people and hear the roar of the bloodthirsty audience as the Gatekeeper flew closer.

"Where are you taking me?" Sinbad yelled over the rushing wind.

"You have qualified for the Tournament Fantastic. I am taking you to meet Lord Yar. He insists on examining each of the new fighters," the Gatekeeper yelled back.

Looking at the ground below, Sinbad saw an epic battle taking place between a centaur and a griffin. The battle was intense, both creatures lunging for each other's throats. The griffin was attempting to claw at the centaur's neck, while the beast reared back and kicked its opponent away with its hooves. The battleground was soaked with blood, some old, and some fresh.

"Lord Yar will be pleased," the humanoid raven said, "...a human has never had the courage or ability to participate in the battles. You will be a first, Sinbad."

Sinbad was not comforted by this.

The Gatekeeper placed Sinbad down on a muted, tile floor. The open, airy room, lined with marble columns, had begun to reflect the first rays of a majestic sunset. Sinbad studied the carvings on the walls, all of them were depictions of violence and conflict. The birdman landed gently beside Sinbad and motioned him towards a bald, lean man sitting on a golden, jewel encrusted throne.

"Follow me, and do not speak unless spoken to. Lord Yar is... well, you will find out for yourself," the Gatekeeper said, and Sinbad had the feeling that no fondness existed between the two.

Sinbad's theory was proven correct as they advanced towards Lord Yar. "Gatekeeper!" Lord Yar yelled with a shrill voice. He turned to face the gigantic raven-man, and Sinbad beheld his appearance. Bald, radiant blue eyes and the most garish clothing that Sinbad had seen outside of a cheap brothel. Each finger held a massive ring, and he wore many ornate necklaces about his person. The treasures Lord Yar adorned himself with appeared to be genuine, but Sinbad wondered how one man could have such expensive garments and yet appear to look so cheap. "I told you not to interrupt me during a match!" he said in a reprimanding voice to the Gatekeeper.

"Another fighter has proven himself worthy of the tournament. This one is a human." The Gatekeeper said, and Sinbad could see much bitterness in the birdman's eyes.

"A new fighter? Why did you not say so before?" Lord Yar asked, then he waved Sinbad over, "Come, let me have a look at you, and see where we will place you in the tournament."

Sinbad walked past the Gatekeeper and stood in front of Lord Yar, but his eyes darted immediately to the crystal that was imbedded in Lord Yar's throne. Sinbad's eyes widened, his goal was only a few feet from him! Nevertheless, he needed to have self-control and restraint, so he looked Lord Yar in the eyes. This, however, was a mistake.

"Since when do lowly fighters get the privilege of looking into the eyes of Lords?!" the despot spat. "Look at the floor when I address you! Were you raised with no common sense, you cur?"

Sinbad did as he was told, and Lord Yar examined him, making a theatrical show of appraising the sailor. He turned to the raven-man and cleared his throat, "Tell me, Gatekeeper, how well did this one do in combat?"

"He has bested me, sir. I was quite impressed, and no doubt the audience will be as well." The Gatekeeper said, and Sinbad sensed sincerity in the raven-man's voice.

"Bested you, you say? You may be losing your touch, Gatekeeper..." Lord Yar said, with what Sinbad assumed the Lord thought was a charming smile.

Turning his gaze back to Sinbad, Lord Yar then countered "...or this one might be a damned fine warrior. Tell me your name, cur, in order that I may bestow upon you a fitting title."

"My name is Sinbad El Ari, my lord." Sinbad spoke plainly, his head still lowered.

"Sinbad! My, my, my... it seems that my little Tournament Fantastic has attracted a living legend. The crowds will love that we now have the famous adventurer among us! I was considering that your first bout would be against the Skeleton, but he now seems inadequate for the likes of you. I will invent something more creative for you in the morning."

"May I ask a question?" Sinbad spoke as respectfully as he could. Nevertheless, Lord Yar looked aghast.

"You may be something of an adventurer, Sinbad, but you forget to whom you are speaking!" Lord Yar bellowed, and Sinbad felt several specks of saliva flick onto his face. "Nevertheless, I find myself curious as to what your question will be. Speak it, Sinbad."

"My lord, what prize am I to claim when I win the Tournament Fantastic?" Sinbad said, his eyes still firmly directed at the tile floor.

"Well, aren't you the confident one, Sinbad!" Lord Yar's laugh was hollow and insincere, "...assuming that you are able to slay my menagerie of monsters, you would be granted your freedom, and a little token from my personal horde of treasures. Anything you desire, Sinbad. I am in a generous mood for some reason."

"What about that crystal?" Sinbad asked, pointing to the jewel embedded in the throne. Though Sinbad's neck was bent down, his eyes shifted to see Lord Yar's expression drop. At first he looked shocked, then a tremendous rage washed over his face and he bellowed.

"The crystal is mine, Sinbad! I will never let it out of my sight! Never!"

Although Lord Yar seemed to covet his many valuables, Sinbad could not help but wonder why he was so attached to this single piece. Did he have knowledge of the crystal's healing abilities?

"I ought to kill you where you stand, Sinbad, and have the Gatekeeper here feast on your rotting corpse." Lord Yar said, regaining his sense of calm, but not bothering to hide his anger. The Gatekeeper looked down, and Sinbad saw that the thought of eating a corpse did not appeal to the raven-human.

Lord Yar's gruesome musings were broken off by the thunderous roar of the crowd. Lord Yar stood up, and Sinbad turned around to see that the griffin had landed the killing blow on the centaur's neck. The centaur lay on the sand, blood flowing from its lifeless body. The griffin screeched, and despite its injuries, pranced triumphantly around the perimeter of the arena.

"Damn! I missed the kill!" Lord Yar said, striking the arm of his golden throne. "Gatekeeper, summon the attendants to take Sinbad to stable four. He can watch the final match of the day." Lord Yar waved Sinbad away, as if he were brushing away an annoying fly.

The Gatekeeper walked away and squawked loudly. Moments later, another raven-human came over, this one looked to be a female, clad in a simple robe. She approached Sinbad and he accompanied her. Sinbad looked back at the arena and saw that the centaur's corpse was being dragged off by other raven-men attendants. Sinbad leaned over to the bird-woman and asked "Your people work for Lord Yar?"

"Work, yes. To death. Lord Yar has enslaved our people, and lets us eat the corpses of those that lose in the tournament." She said in a whisper, and Sinbad nodded grimly. "Lord Yar had our warriors killed, and the one he calls the Gatekeeper is the only one left."

"What did Lord Yar mean by stable four?"

"It is where he keeps the fighters between matches. They eat and sleep there, their only window is a view of the arena." She replied with a mournful note in her voice.

Though Sinbad's head was swimming with questions, he decided not to press any further. He had to formulate a plan. He needed to escape, that was for certain, but the crystal was not to be the prize that Krassa had told him. Sinbad could not escape without that crystal, but he had no idea of how to get past Lord Yar.

The female raven-human stopped at the edge of a rusted, wrought iron door, and opened it with a key that was attached to her leather belt. "Here are your quarters," she said in a tone that suggested that she had spoken these words to a thousand fallen fighters, "...rest well, Lord Yar will announce when you will be fighting. Your dinner will be served after the upcoming battle."

Sinbad entered the stable, and was greeted by a depressing sight. "The stable" as Lord Yar had appropriately labeled it, was a large, stone room with hay strewn about on the floor. Sinbad noticed the dried blood on the floor, and observed that there were no beds or accommodations of any kind. Various fighters had piled hay into makeshift beds, and the only light available was provided by a large, barred door. Sinbad surmised that the window also served as the entrance and exit to the arena.

His companions were an animated skeleton, whose bones bore several scratches and notches in them. Sinbad assumed that this being was a veteran of many battles. There was an exotic creature that Sinbad had never seen before, but he had heard tales of the Lamassu. It had the body of a lion, massive wings of an eagle (which were bound by a painful looking leather harness) and an androgynous human head. Several raven-people were nursing its wounds, which looked to be severe.

"Please, be gentle..." the Lamassu urged. It was not being rude to its attendants, but it was suffering. The raven-people understood as they kept working.

"Well, well, well..." a deep, thunderous voice boomed from a dark corner of the room. Sinbad, awed by the sight of his new companions, had not noticed this one. As soon as the hulking figure stood, Sinbad recognized the beast as a Minotaur, and though it was difficult to read expressions on a bull's face, he could detect that the beast was not impressed. "We have a human here at last..." the Minotaur continued, "and a pathetic one at that. I could crush your skull in my hands!" The beast declared as he put his large, thick hands to the sides of Sinbad's head, most likely for dramatic effect. Though the Minotaur was at least twelve feet tall, Sinbad felt that he had little to fear from this beast.

"For all your talk, I'd like to see you fight. Then I may be impressed, though I doubt it." Sinbad said, egging the Minotaur on. He saw the beast's eyes grow large with rage, and it raised a hand to strike Sinbad. Although Sinbad was ready to dodge the blow, the Skeleton had leapt up and placed a dagger to the Minotaur's inner thigh.

"From what I understand of flesh creatures, slicing here will cause them to lose much blood and cripple them, correct?" the Skeleton spoke in an elegant, though slightly raspy tone. The Minotaur paused as it felt a cold, sharpened dagger against its leg. "I suggest you leave our new friend alone, and concentrate on your upcoming battle. 'Tis not to be an easy one, if Lord Yar sticks to his plan."

The Minotaur held his pose, weighing his options mentally, before dropping his arm and grumbling as he went back to his corner. Sinbad turned to the Skeleton, who was shuffling back to his. "I owe you, my friend. Pray tell me your name?" Sinbad said as he extended his hand. The Skeleton looked at it, and reluctantly clasped him about the arm.

"My name... has been lost to me... I only have vague memories of battles from another time... Lord Yar calls me Skeleton. Forgive my hesitation on your gesture of friendship, for I am reluctant to make a friend that I might soon lose."

"I can understand, Skeleton. My name is Sinbad El Ari, and Lord Yar had considered that I might do battle with you. However, his mind seems to have changed." Sinbad said, and after seeing the lightning quick reflexes that

Skeleton has just displayed, he felt relieved.

"Huh..." Skeleton grunted, "...I have heard of your many voyages, Sinbad. You would have been a challenging opponent." Skeleton carefully hid his dagger in his stack of hay as he asked, "So, how did he persuade you to come here?"

"I never met Lord Yar until today... I was sent on a mission by..." Sinbad started to speak, but Skeleton held up his hand in order to silence the adventurer.

"Let me guess... Krassa!"

"You know him?" Sinbad exclaimed in bewilderment.

"Of course, he lied to all of us to get us to this wretched Tournament Fantastic! He promised me that my past would be revealed and my memories restored. If I were able to acquire this mysterious crystal," Skeleton replied with a dark edge to his voice.

"I was separated from my tribe," the Lamassu said. "Krassa claimed that he was a wandering magician and that I would be able to find my way home once I won the crystal from the tournament." The raven-people looked on the prisoners with great pity.

"Then the Sultan is... he is condemned to death," Sinbad said, feeling everything within him sink. "The crystal is useless!"

"Not quite useless," the Skeleton said. "Lord Yar covets it, and I do not doubt that it has magical properties. I can sense it."

"You can sense magic?" Sinbad asked. Though he felt defeated, Sinbad was determined to escape the island and hunt down Krassa for his treachery, but Skeleton's statement about the crystal's magic had made the adventurer curious and hopeful.

Their conversation was cut short by Lord Yar's voice. Sinbad had thought that his voice was unpleasant in person, but it became much more irritating as it bellowed out over the arena. "What a thrilling battle that was between the Griffin and the Centaur, but that is about to be overshadowed by the climactic battle of the evening! Now we will watch as the mighty Minotaur fights the brutal Basilisk! Who will win? Let us find out!"

The Minotaur stood up, pounding his fists together with a look of glee on his face. He turned to Sinbad with a smug expression. "Watch, human, and you will see how a battle is won."

The gate opened and the Minotaur strode out to face a screaming crowd. He stretched his broad, muscular arms wide, addressing his adoring fans. The Basilisk slithered out of his pit on the opposite side of the arena. Its emerald green scales glimmered against the evening sky. The serpent's large, amber eyes, Sinbad remembered, were imbued with a deadly kind of magic that could turn whatever made eye-contact with the Basilisk's gaze into stone. Flicking its tongue, the serpent studied its new environment as it waited for the Minotaur to attack. The great serpent, despite its tremendous size, was just as swift as its smaller cousins. The Basilisk locked eyes with the Minotaur, hoping to end the fight quickly by turning the immense man-bull to stone.

The Minotaur, however, had anticipated this strategy and planned a counter-attack. The Minotaur closed its eyes, thereby nullifying the gigantic serpent's magic, and charged at the Basilisk with incredible ferocity. The earth shook beneath the Minotaur's hooves as the crowd roared, egging them on, demanding to see blood. Sinbad, for his part, cheered as well, though it was on behalf of the Basilisk. He was beginning to formulate a plan to steal the crystal and escape, and the Basilisk could help him immensely.

It was to Sinbad's horror that the Basilisk was gored by the long, battle-scarred bull horns of the Minotaur. His midsection pierced, the Basilisk screamed in pain, and the audience enjoyed every second of the beast's agony. The injury, though grievous, did not prove fatal, and the Basilisk retaliated. Bending its neck, the Basilisk opened its mouth wide and sank its fangs deep into the Minotaur's back. It was the Minotaur's turn to cry out in pain, much to the approval of the crowd. Sinbad gave an encouraging yell, as did everyone else in the pit. If the Minotaur was dispatched, all the better for them.

The Minotaur dislodged its horns from the Basilisk, stumbling backwards as it did so. The Basilisk shifted its serpentine body in order to hide its gaping wounds from the Minotaur. This brought its head down to the Minotaur's reach, and the bull-man attempted to strike his opponent with its gigantic, granite-hard fists. The Basilisk proved too swift, it bobbed and weaved its head, almost tauntingly, out of the Minotaur's reach. The Minotaur was only swinging with one hand, using the other to shield his eyes. This left a vulnerable spot for the Basilisk to exploit, and it kept biting the Minotaur with each missed swing.

Growing frustrated, the Minotaur leapt at the Basilisk. Instead of using his horns as weapons, the Minotaur seized the serpent about its writhing body and, with incredible effort, hurled the beast over his head!

The Basilisk landed near Sinbad's stable, and the adventurer could sense that the beast was in great pain. Though obviously not human, Sinbad could detect a sense of determination on the great snake's face. The Basilisk curled up once more to face his opponent. It sniffed the air with its tongue and let out what could best be described as a laugh.

The Minotaur had not moved from his position across the arena, in fact, the beast was standing in place, wobbling unsteadily on its hooves. Suddenly, the beast dropped to the earth with a resounding thud. The audience seemed stunned, but Sinbad had deduced what had taken place; the Basilisk's venom had poisoned the Minotaur and had killed it. Soon the silence was broken by

"...THE MINOTAUR LEAPT AT THE BASILISK..."

either applause and cheers or cries of outrage from the audience. The Raven-men came and escorted the Basilisk to Sinbad's stable.

Out of respect, the titanic snake closed its eyes as it rested in its new chambers. It flicked out its tongue and began looking around curiously.

"Yes, it is a human." The Lamassu said to the Basilisk, and somehow the serpent could understand it. "His name is Sinbad."

The Basilisk made a strange, but oddly pleasant hissing noise.

"She gives her greetings, but asks that you let her rest from the battle." The Lamassu translated, and then explained, "I understand all languages."

"I see, that is certainly useful," Sinbad said, before addressing the room. "Has anyone or anything ever attempted to escape?" he asked.

"Yes, but a powerful magic protects the arena and Lord Yar's quarters. Only the audience is allowed to enter and leave." Skeleton said.

"I may have a plan, but I need to know more..." Sinbad started to say, but Lamassu stopped him.

"Sinbad, you are tired and need rest. Unless I am mistaken, Lord Yar will have you fight in the morning. Conserve your strength and we will talk later."

Though he was desperate for action, Sinbad saw the wisdom of the Lamassu's words and decided to sleep, though he desired nothing more than to plan his escape with the crystal. The Basilisk had taken residence in the Minotaur's former corner, so Sinbad rested on what little hay he could find.

His dreams were tormented by visions of the Sultan dying, feverishly crying out for Sinbad, wondering where he was.

Sinbad woke with the dawning of the sun and saw that he was the first to rise in the stable. He was groggy, and gently brushed off some hay that had stuck to his clothing. His muscles were sore from his fight with the Gatekeeper, and his shoulders ached from the raven-man's iron grip. Clearing his head as he rose, Sinbad looked at the sleeping creatures around him, careful not to disturb them as he got to his feet. His goal would be impossible to accomplish alone. Sinbad knew that he needed to get a message to his crew. There was no doubt in his mind that every creature here, himself included, was treated like a prisoner. Lord Yar would not allow for outside communication. Yet there had to be a way.

The door to the stable opened, and despite the attempt to quiet the creaking, it echoed throughout the chamber. The female raven-human that lead Sinbad into the stable peaked in, carrying what looked to be a tray of food. Seeing that Sinbad was already awake, she crept over and handed the tray to him.

"I was about to wake everyone here. It is time for your morning meal. The meals cater to every species. This is yours, and I hope it is to your satisfaction," she said.

"Tell me, what is your name?" Sinbad inquired as he grabbed a bread roll from his tray. Though the food portions were meager, they were designed with health in mind: root vegetables, a small helping of rice, bread rolls, and several slices of meat with gravy.

"My... name?" she said haltingly.

"Yes. Mine is Sinbad El Ari. What is yours?" he repeated, offering her a smile to win her trust.

"We, as a culture, do not have names. Traditionally, we have special calls for one another. Only my husband has a name; The Gatekeeper," she explained.

"The Gatekeeper? That is your husband!" Sinbad exclaimed, surprised. The Skeleton began to stir, and Sinbad realized that he spoke too loudly. The Basilisk too began to move, her tongue flicking as she smelled the morning air (and Sinbad's meal).

"Yes. Lord Yar deems it necessary to keep us apart. This ensures that my husband will obey. I miss him so," she said sadly as she turned her back on Sinbad. It was then that Sinbad noticed that the raven-woman had a harness on her wings, much like the Lamassu, preventing them from spreading.

"Raveness..." Sinbad blurted out, and she turned to him with a look of interest on her face.

"So that is my name, according to you?" she asked.

"Well, it will have to do, for I must call you something," Sinbad said by way of explanation.

"You're not terribly creative, are you?" Skeleton said as he rose to his feet.

"I was forced to invent on the spur of the moment," Sinbad shrugged. "But Raveness, why do you and the Lamassu not break free of your bonds and escape?"

"Because Krassa, Lord Yar's servant, has placed a magic spell on the bonds which prevents anyone from removing them," Raveness explained, and the Lamassu, now awake, nodded in agreement. "Only Krassa, or perhaps a magical blade, can remove them."

"Indeed, one of my crew is in possession of such a weapon, but I need to get a message to them saying where I am!" Sinbad said. Then an idea occurred to him, "Raveness, since the Gatekeeper is the only being to venture back and forth between the Tournament Fantastic, would you be willing to pass a message along to your husband?"

"He comes here for a meal, so I would be willing to. But how can I trust you?" Raveness asked with a suspicious gleam in her eye.

"What do you mean?" Sinbad replied, beginning to feel defensive. "I am the legendary sailor, Sinbad! My voyages..."

"How am I to know that you are not some cruel test of Lord Yar's? He may be attempting to test my loyalty. And you, Sinbad, have killed many creatures, treating them as monsters. Why should any of us show you loyalty?" Raveness said. Though her voice was gentle, her conviction was firm. Sinbad was about to reply, but thought before he spoke.

"I will prove to you that I am not the monster you think I am. Watch me in the arena today, all of you." Sinbad swept his arm across the stable, to indicate every creature he was imprisoned with. The Basilisk reared up and hissed at him in a threatening tone. Sinbad did not expect his proclamation to be welcome, but felt himself shudder at her fearsome sound.

"Be that as it may," the Lamassu began as it started to translate. "The Basilisk is unhappy. You are preventing the young woman from fetching its meal because of your conversation."

"I am sorry, forgive my selfishness!" Sinbad said as Raveness scurried out of the room and opened the gate. Though the Basilisk kept her eyes closed, she gave a low, threatening hiss at Sinbad as she slithered out into the open.

"The Basilisk is allowed to roam free?" Sinbad questioned.

"Yes, feeding her is quite the chore. Lord Yar deemed it wiser for her to feast on the corpses that the raven-people do not consume." The Lamassu explained wearily. Sinbad, however, was beginning to form a plan, but several factors remained great unknowns to the sailor.

"Who are these spectators? Where do they come from and where do they live between matches?" Sinbad asked the Lamassu.

"When Krassa tricked me into coming here, I saw that there was an encampment outside the arena. I assume that the crowd retires there between battles." The beast explained, recalling the events with a mournful look on his face.

"I may have a plan to free us all provided that I can get a message to my crew," Sinbad said, but Skeleton shook his head.

"You and every other new combatant have uttered those same hollow words. Krassa and Lord Yar have planned for every eventuality," Skeleton said cynically.

The adventurer moved towards Skeleton who was pacing back and forth in his small corner, ready for a confrontation.

"Your temperament will be of no help if we are to escape, friend," Sinbad said with a sternness in his voice. Though he was no longer aboard his ship, Sinbad was a born leader, and his instincts for command were taking over.

"I understand that you may be famous, but you still have to prove yourself to us. I think I can speak for all of the combatants when I say that we will not follow you blindly," Skeleton said through gritted teeth.

"I will prove myself, do not doubt that, Skeleton. But why the reluctance? With your nature, I assumed that you would have viewed death as some merciful release." Sinbad challenged the Skeleton's position.

"No, not before I find out who I was," Skeleton said, as a current of fear ran through his voice. "And why I am here."

Raveness came back, dragging a wooden box of food behind her. Sinbad observed that the food, though it was cooked, was mostly thrown together. It consisted of meat, starches, and vegetables, everything Lord Yar assumed that his fighters would need.

"Divide this amongst yourselves, as per usual," she said with a solemn note in her voice. "Sinbad, you fight after breakfast, so I suggest eating lightly." Sinbad nodded grimly, then Raveness approached him with a determined look in her eye, "Remember your promise, Sinbad. Prove that you are not a monster and we will follow you."

"And will you pass a message along to your husband?" Sinbad inquired with a tense expression on his face. His entire plan of escape, and saving the Sultan, depended on her answer. Raveness seemed to read this in his expression, and sighed thoughtfully.

"Yes, if you prove yourself to me," Raveness said as she left the room, hurrying to attend to her other duties.

The Skeleton declined food, pointing out that it was unnecessary for him to eat. Sinbad divided the food between him and the Lamassu, giving the winged creature a larger portion. Sinbad ate his stew dispassionately, his mind back to the Blue Nymph. He was thinking of the message he planned to compose for his crew. His thoughts were interrupted by the Skeleton giving a sardonic laugh.

"Sinbad, if ever there was a creature that you needed to prove yourself worthy of..." the Skeleton laughed, "I can see the ravens trying to wrangle him now. If you want to take a look."

Sinbad went to the Skeleton as he pointed his bony arm at the opposite side of the arena. Sinbad's jaw dropped! What he saw was a figure resembling a man, at least eight feet tall, struggling against the chains that the raven-people were pulling. His entire body appeared to be made of black, marbled stone. Though its expression was frozen, as if etched into a rock, a fury radiated from it, as it swatted a raven-man with a brutal swipe.

"Sinbad, that is a Golem. Like me, it is a spirit trapped in a physical form. Unlike me, he is bitter about it," Skeleton explained as he watched the creature struggle. "Keep in mind, that like me, the Golem does not tire nor feel pain."

"I will defeat him, but I will not kill him, this I vow," Sinbad said, mustering a confident voice that he certainly did not feel inside.

"Good luck defeating him in the first place!" The Skeleton laughed amusingly at Sinbad's bravado.

"What weapons am I allowed?" Sinbad asked the Lamassu, for he was growing tired of the sadistic pleasure that the Skeleton was getting in taunting him.

"None. Lord Yar feels that the only fair fight is one without the aid of weapons. Claw to claw, fang to fang, hand to hand," the Lamassu said apologetically, knowing that Sinbad would be horrified at this reveal.

"How am I supposed to defeat a man of stone with my bare hands?" Sinbad exclaimed.

"Good question," Skeleton laughed as he went back to his corner, leaving Sinbad alone to contemplate his strategy.

"But remember!" Skeleton said, catching Sinbad off guard. "Take heed of the old expression, the bigger they are, the harder they fall."

His heart pounding in his chest, Sinbad strode out into the arena. His feet sank into the deep sand as he watched the Golem stand stoically at the opposite end of the arena. A gentle breeze carried a wave of sand that swirled around him. Sinbad began to look around for anything that could be used as a weapon against the stone giant. He saw the crowd gathered in the stands, a cacophony of screaming bloodlust filled the air. The blazing sun beat down upon the arena and made Sinbad sweat, yet he stood defiantly, attempting to mask his fear of the Golem.

As Sinbad cast his gaze around the arena, he saw Lord Yar sitting pompously on his throne. Even at this distance, Sinbad could see Lord Yar's expression. He looked gleeful, excited at the prospect of the sailor being smashed to pieces by the Golem. Sinbad vowed to wipe the smug expression off his face forever. Just as Sinbad was about to focus on his gigantic opponent, he saw another figure step up to the side of Lord Yar's throne. It was Krassa! The alchemist was watching Sinbad as well, and gave the sailor a "friendly" wave of the hand.

"Well," thought Sinbad. "He,ar too shall pay! But I have greater problems to contend with first."

Sinbad and the Golem locked eyes; its lumbering gate began sending small blasts of sand up in the air as the stone beast advanced. Sinbad weighed his options: striking the Golem would only shatter his hand, and he had no weapons to speak of. Sinbad surmised that his comment about taking Lord

Yar's crystal had upset the despot greatly, so much so that he had set the adventurer an impossible challenge.

"No! There has to be a way!" Sinbad thought to himself. The Sultan's life was in his hands, and he was not about to fail! There must be some way to defeat, yet not slay the Golem. Sinbad had remembered his vow to his fellow combatants, and desperately needed to gain their trust if he was to save the Sultan.

The Golem moved slowly towards Sinbad. His monstrous motion slowed down as the spirit within the creature struggled to animate the stone body that it was bound to. The adventurer thought that he could use his agility to his advantage, but had no idea of how to exploit it. Suddenly, the Golem brought his fist down to crush Sinbad. Sinbad instinctively dove out of the way as a geyser of sand erupted from the Golem's fist as it struck the arena floor.

Rolling into a crouching position, Sinbad noticed that the Golem was frozen in its pose, struggling to recover its balance. Then he thought of the Skeleton's advice and realized what it meant. Sinbad pulled off his leather vest and twisted the garment in his hands. Gripping it tightly, he flung one end of the vest around the stone leg of the Golem and caught the empty armhole with his free hand. The crowd became silent, curious as to what Sinbad was planning.

Digging his heels into the sand, Sinbad pulled and yanked against the Golem's supporting leg with all of his might. His arms tensed and his taut muscles vibrated. Sinbad gritted his teeth and he saw the Golem's foot finally slide towards him. The stone beast realized what Sinbad's plan was and attempted to adjust its balance, but it was to no avail.

With one final, exhausting yank, Sinbad managed to slip the Golem's supporting leg out from underneath him, causing the giant to collapse into the firmly packed sand. It flung its arms forward to brace itself against the ground, but the exertion was too much for its stone body, and the Golem's arms shattered upon impact. Seizing the opportunity, Sinbad, though exhausted, leapt onto the back of the fallen creature and bellowed at Lord Yar and Krassa.

"His arms are broken! The Golem has not the strength to continue fighting, nor does he possess the muscles necessary bring himself to his feet. Therefore, this match is over! I am the victor!" Sinbad saw Lord Yar glance with uncertainty over to Krassa, who shook his head. Lord Yar stood up and approached the balcony, ready to address the crowd. Sensing that the cruel despot was not about to end the match, Sinbad improvised. Turning to the crowd, Sinbad shouted to them, "What say you?"

The crowd erupted into thunderous applause, much to the displeasure of Lord Yar. Sinbad had counted on the fact that Lord Yar would rather die than disappoint his crowd. Sinbad saw Lord Yar raise his hands to settle the masses, who were now exultingly shouting the name "Sinbad!"

"This match has concluded," Lord Yar said with great reluctance, though he did his best to appear regal and contained. Lord Yar dismissively waved his hand towards the stable. The sailor took some delight in Lord Yar's snarling face. This was the first battle he won against Lord Yar. His next move was entirely dependent on the judgment of Raveness.

The gate to his stable was opened, and Sinbad wearily strode inside. He saw the Basilisk, Lamassu, Skeleton and Raveness watching him with great interest. The sailor's eyes, however, were on Ravness, and he was apprehensive upon seeing her folded arms, and the glare in her eyes. Sinbad was expecting trouble.

"I did not kill it," he ventured, curious to see how Raveness would react to his statement.

"Yes, but you have crippled him, which some would consider to be worse," Raveness replied tersely.

"Magic may yet heal the Golem's arms and that beast offered me no quarter or mercy, if you will recall," Sinbad pointed out.

The Lamassu turned to Raveness and spoke in an eloquent tone. "I understand why you would be fearful of trusting a human. They have shown us nothing but contempt and cruelty. However, this one, Sinbad El Ari, did complete the challenge you set before him. It would be dishonorable to break your promise to the man."

Raveness thought to argue, but then she sighed. The Lamassu's logic outweighed her feelings, and it seemed as if the others would support Sinbad. Giving Sinbad a defeated gaze, she asked, "All you would have me do is deliver a message?"

"Yes. I have devised a plan in which all of us, all of the imprisoned creatures, may be free from Lord Yar and Krassa's cruelty, but I cannot do this alone. I need the aid of my crew." Sinbad turned his eyes from Raveness and looked at the rest of the combatants. "And your help as well."

"I knew *that* was coming," Skeleton grumbled.

Sinbad then told them of his plan.

Tishimi Osara did not frighten easily. She was a battle-hardened warrior who had lived through a lifetime of tragedy. She, along with the rest of the crew of the Blue Nymph, worried about Sinbad. It had been two days since he set foot on the island. Though there was much talk of sending a rescue party, no decision had been made. In an attempt to divert her thoughts, Tishimi practiced a kata with her magical katana on deck. It was a routine that she had mastered early in her samurai training, and Tishimi hoped that the simplicity of the form would help her focus her thoughts.

So focused was she on her body movements, that Tishimi was unaware of the large Raven-man flying towards the Blue Nymph. The Gatekeeper landed in front of her, giving Tishimi quite a start. Ralf gave a cry of alarm and soon the crew of the Blue Nymph were scrambling for their weapons. Tishimi, however, was closest to the Gatekeeper, and though she was ready to attack, she sensed that the large, broad-shouldered creature did not come for a fight.

The Gatekeeper raised his voice, drowning out the frantic cries of the Blue Nymph's crew. "I do not wish to fight. I come bearing a message from your captain, Sinbad!"

"What sort of message?" William Byrne asked. He was the first to recover from the initial shock of seeing the Gatekeeper, but he still held his sword. The raven-man looked at Sinbad's crew, knowing that his next words were critical.

"He has devised a plan which will help him escape."

Thus, the Gatekeeper was taken below deck, where he explained in great detail the strategy that Sinbad had set forth. Henri, to no one's surprise, was the first to grumble.

"Evidently his time in Lord Yar's arena has driven him quite mad! It is utter lunacy at best and suicidal at worst. I think I would prefer to guard the ship."

"Oh, *there's* a surprise!" Ralf growled through gritted teeth. "Tishimi here will be getting the lion's share of the danger, and you do not hear her belly aching!"

"Well she hardly speaks in the first place," Henri said defensively.

Tishimi had listened closely to the plan, and realized that while the others in the crew were needed purely for muscle, she was needed for a far greater purpose. Ralf was not exaggerating; she would be in more danger than the rest of the crew, having to place her trust in a wild beast that she had never set eyes on. However, her loyalty to her captain outweighed any fear that she felt about this mission.

"I accept," Tishimi said, looking into the Gatekeeper's eyes.

"Sure, now she speaks just to spite me," Henri said sarcastically as he crossed his arms.

The rest of the crew, inspired by Tishimi, soon agreed to the madcap plan. The Gatekeeper was pleased. He and Tishimi moved towards the mast of the ship while he spoke privately to her.

"I am thankful for your decision. If your captain's plan succeeds, then my wife and I can live in happiness once again."

"I will not fail either of you," Tishimi vowed as she stretched her arms out from her sides. The Gatekeeper placed his muscular arms around the samurai and flew from the deck towards the island. William, Henri, and Ralf went ashore while Omar took charge of the ship in Sinbad's absence.

The Gatekeeper set down with Tishimi close to Lord Yar's arena. It was in a mountainous region, and Tishimi could see a large encampment on a cliff nearby. The Gatekeeper had explained to Tishimi that that was where the spectators dwelled between tournament bouts. He could not risk being seen by them, for that could raise suspicion and alert Lord Yar to that fact that something was amiss. Tishimi had to silently make her way to the Basilisk's feeding pit, where the first step in Sinbad's plan was to take place.

Tishimi approached the edge of the pit, where a disgusting mound of dead creatures was unceremoniously pushed to the center. It was to be the Basilisk's meal. This feast was "prepared" by two of Lord Yar's men, humans that Tishimi overheard making crude remarks and comments about the corpses and the Basilisk. One perched himself on the edge of the pit, while the other started to hand crank a lever that opened the gate. The mechanism was loud, and it masked the sound of Timishi sneaking up behind the sitting henchman.

"I do not mind telling you that I hate those damn bird people of Lord Yars, " the sitting henchman began to complain to his friend, "I mean, they get the easy jobs of serving him food and wine. Fetch this, fetch that, and we're stuck here feeding corpses to a giant snake!"

"Well, you know Lord Yar's attitude; keep your enemies closer and all that. I imagine that he likes to keep an eye on all those damn birds." The second henchman replied as the gate began to rise. The hissing and heavy breathing of the Basilisk was growing louder and closer.

"Yeah, well if they ever try to rebel or anything, I hope he pays us extra when we cut their lousy heads off."

"Yeah, well, I know I do *not* get paid nearly enough to listen to your whimpering day in and day out!" the henchman said as he strained against the gears. He was expecting a reply, as he was accustomed to hearing his partner's constant jibes and complaints. However, nothing came. He finished opening the gate and locked it into position, turning his back on the Basilisk as he looked for his now silent friend.

"Where are you?" were the last words the henchman would ever speak. An expert slash from Tishimi's katana saw to that.

Tishimi slid down to the bottom of the pit and faced the Basilisk as it slithered towards her. Closing her eyes and bracing herself, she felt the Basilisk's breath and the titanic snake's mouth close around her.

"TISHIMI... FACED THE BASILISK..."

"So you really think this will work?" The Skeleton asked Sinbad, a disgruntled sigh in his voice. He watched as the sailor was stretching and limbering up his muscles to get himself ready for action. In a few moments, Sinbad would find out if his plan would come to fruition. Or he would find out if he had squandered his life, the life of one of his crewmates, and the Sultan. The Skeleton's questions and cynical attitude were not aiding him in his attempts to relax.

"It must," Sinbad said as he practiced a few kicks, "for I have no other options. Now, are you prepared to do your part?"

"Yes, yes... assuming that we get that far," the Skeleton said as he stood up and stared fixedly at Sinbad. Sinbad could not help but shake the eerie knowledge that a being with literally no eyes was attempting to stare him down.

"We will, my friend. In a matter of moments," Sinbad began, feigning a confidence in his strategy that he did not feel inside.

"Silence!" The Lamassu interrupted. The two turned to see the door to their stable slowly rise, as the Basilisk slithered back into its corner. The guards paid no heed to the snake, but Sinbad's heart was racing. It was now the moment of truth and his plan depended entirely on what happened next.

"Well!" Sinbad snapped at the colossal serpent, for he found the tension unbearable. The great snake raised its head and slowly, carefully opened its mouth. Tishimi quickly jumped out, and began to furiously wipe the Basilisk's saliva from her body. The Skeleton's jaw dropped.

"The loyalty you inspire... Sinbad... well, let's just say that I would have never stowed away in the mouth of a Basilisk!" The Skeleton said.

"It was the only way I could think of to get Tishimi and her magic sword inside without alerting the guards," Sinbad said as he made his way towards the female samurai. She offered him a glare.

"Now that I am here, Captain, tell me what must be done next," Tishimi said. Despite her obvious anger at the method of transportation, she remained a loyal professional who would follow her leader to the end.

"Now that the first step has been completed, we will proceed to the most difficult part. Tishimi will use her blade to sever the enchanted bindings around the Lamassu's wings," Sinbad explained.

Nodding, the samurai strode over to the Lamassu and with one swift stroke of her sword, she sliced the magical harness that bound the Lamassu's wings and prevented the creature from flying. With a look of tremendous relief on its face, the beast stretched and flexed its wings for the first time in a long while. The others in the stable, even the Skeleton, looked delighted to see the Lamassu's overwhelming happiness.

Though Sinbad too was basking in the Lamassu's joy, he forced himself to divert his attention to the door, where the next step in his escape plan was to take place. The two guards assigned to his stable were asleep, as usual. Thus, they were unable to see the large, brawny forms of Ralf and William approaching them. The Viking grabbed the guard nearest him and with one swift movement broke the guard's neck like a twig. At the same time, William slid a dagger from his belt and plunged it into the other guard. The two had taken an unsecured route that the Gatekeeper had described to them, and now were in a very precarious position. If they were spotted as they attempted to open the door to Sinbad's stable, all would be for not. Using his tremendous might, Ralf began to rotate the wheel that opened the door. Even when William jumped in to help, it seemed to Sinbad as if it would take an eternity for the gate to fully rise.

Then, to their horror, a lone guard, returning from the mess hall to bring the two guards a flask of wine, spotted them! Everyone stood motionless, unsure of who was going to make the first move. Overcoming his shock, the guard cupped his hands to his mouth and started to yell.

But his yell was cut short by an arrow to his diaphragm. What was to be a booming, echoing call for help turned into nothing more than a small gurgle as the guard dropped to the sand, the flask landing beside him. A moment later, Henri had leapt from one of the walls and landed near the fallen guard, the arena's sand cushioning his impact. Snatching the flask from the ground, Henri took a generous swig as he dragged the guard's body towards the others.

"I will say this for Lord Yar, at least he has an exquisite taste in wine," Henri said as he looked at the flask. "Come now, you're wasting time marveling at my heroic rescue."

"If there is one thing worse than his constant whining," Ralf grumbled to William as he continued opening the gate, "it is his endless boasting."

A short while later, the gate was opened. The final and most important step in Sinbad's escape was to take place. The Basilisk, William, Henri, Tishimi and Ralf were to free the other combatants and cause as much chaos as they could in order to keep Lord Yar's guards busy. The Gatekeeper and Raveness had orders to rally the Raven-people and attack the guards at the spectator's settlement. The Lamassu, with Sinbad and the Skeleton on his back, would fly up to Lord Yar's chambers. There, they would dispatch Lord Yar, and take Krassa and the crystal back to Nesuah to save his life.

"Well..." the Skeleton said as he mounted the Lamassu, wrapping his bony, cold arms around Sinbad, "if this fails, at least it will be spectacular."

"I suppose," Sinbad agreed while resenting the Skeleton's innate talent for filling his mind with doubt.

The Lamassu flew for the first time in a great while, while the others charged out of the stable, fire in their eyes, and war cries screaming from their lips. The other combatants, seeing what was happening, began to cheer as Ralf and William opened their doors. Henri shot down the approaching guards with expertly placed arrows as the Basilisk, lacking arms, simply tore the doors apart with its massive jaw and great fangs. As a small battalion of Lord Yar's men charged at the escaping gladiators, they were met with the chilling amber gaze of the Basilisk. None had time to close their eyes or turn away, and the battalion was transformed from a charging army to a series of stone statues. The menagerie of combatants knocked them to pieces as they stormed the arena, fighting Lord Yar's guards.

"Can someone tell me what the hell is going on out there!" Lord Yar screamed as his attendants hastily strapped his battle armor onto him. Krassa was standing in Lord Yar's chamber as well, with a look of great concern on his face as he nervously wrung his hands together.

"It is the combatants, sir! It seems as if Sinbad is leading them in a revolt!" A guard yelled over the rising sounds of battle.

"Sinbad! Curse him! By this day's end I shall have his head mounted on a pike!" Lord Yar yelled, flailing his arms about, sending his attendants scurrying around in an attempt to finish piecing together his armor.

"He is here for the crystal," Krassa murmured. "Perhaps if we were to give it to him, he would leave and call off the rebellion?"

"Coward!" Lord Yar bellowed. "I will never give that worthless sailor the crystal, never! I would sooner destroy it than let him have that crystal's power! Follow me!" Lord Yar motioned to Krassa as he began to stride out of the room.

"But sir...!" Lord Yar heard one of his attendants yell in protest.

"Later!" Lord Yar yelled as he took his helmet from the armor rack near the door. Facing Krassa, he commanded: "Now, enchant the armor, make it invincible. I command you!"

Making a quick series of motions with his hand, and muttering in a language that had been all but forgotten, Krassa passed his hand over Lord Yar's armor. A magical force attached itself to the armor, and Lord Yar was now invulnerable to attack.

"Let's see that sailor try to steal the crystal from me now!" Lord Yar scoffed as he headed for his throne. Krassa was following behind him with a troubled expression on his face.

The Skeleton and Sinbad dismounted from the Lamassu, and a quick glance around confirmed that Lord Yar and Krassa were nowhere to be found. Sinbad's first thought was to retrieve the crystal, but to his great horror, there was a hole in the throne where the crystal had been! Sinbad turned to the Skeleton and yelled.

"Lord Yar has already taken the crystal!"

"He is not getting away from me!" The Skeleton said through gritted teeth.

"Lamassu, fly around and patrol the outside of the arena. If you spot Lord Yar or Krassa, bring them to us alive!" Sinbad commanded to the great beast.

"Very well," the Lamassu nodded as it soared towards the sky once again.

"Now what do we do?" The Skeleton asked Sinbad. The adventurer was lost for words at the moment, but he heard a voice from the shadows.

"You fool! You have dismissed your strongest fighter!" It was Lord Yar, advancing towards Sinbad. He had his blade drawn in one hand, and the crystal in the other. Krassa was beside him, wearing a false sense of bravado on his face.

"Do anything foolish and you guarantee the Sultan's death!" Lord Yar warned as he gripped the crystal tightly. "With my armor I have the strength to crush this into a handful of dust!"

The Skeleton was slowly moving, trying to maneuver himself into position to strike at Lord Yar. However, Krassa noticed this and began to work a spell on the Skeleton. "You are nothing but a ghost possessing a collection of bones. It should be an easy matter to separate the two!"

Sinbad looked at the Skeleton struggling against Krassa's magic, then to the crystal and Lord Yar. He was trying to see any way to turn the situation to his advantage, but nothing presented itself. He hoped to stall Lord Yar.

"Please tell me, Lord Yar, what is this crystal exactly? Why is it so important?"

"This crystal," Lord Yar began as he looked at it with reverence, "will grant the one who possesses it anything they wish. I wished for this arena and to enslave the raven-people."

"You have what you want? Why keep it?" Sinbad asked, aware of something approaching Lord Yar from behind.

"Why? Because..." Lord Yar's speech was interrupted by a reflection in the crystal. He saw an enormous black raven's eye and turned to see the Gatekeeper standing behind him! The gigantic bird grabbed Lord Yar by the chest and slammed him down on the ground, cracking the tiles where he fell. Raveness was behind her husband, and pounced upon Krassa, her break pecking violently at the dark wizard's neck.

Now that he had broken free from Krassa's curse, the Skeleton saw that the crystal had been flung from Lord Yar's hand during the struggle. Skeleton dove for it. Holding the shimmering rock in his bony hands, the Skeleton held it aloft and whispered: "I wish to remember who I was..."

Suddenly a guard appeared, brandishing a sword. He rushed at Sinbad, but the sailor used the man's own momentum against him. He grabbed hold of the guard's wrist, wrenched the sword from his hand, and threw the man over the ledge. Now armed, Sinbad checked to see who needed help. The Gatekeeper, fueled by vengeance and hatred, was engaged in an intense battle with Lord Yar. Though the birdman was the far superior fighter, Lord Yar's invincible armor kept him alive. The Skeleton was holding onto the crystal, absorbed by its powers. It was then, to his horror, that Sinbad saw Raveness slay Krassa with one final, devastating peck of her beak!

"No!" Sinbad yelled at he rushed over to her, "I told you that I needed him alive to remove the curse from the Sultan! You have doomed him to death!"

Raveness, recovering from the intense rage that overwhelmed her, glanced at Sinbad. She looked aghast. She stammered, "I am sorry. I was just..." Raveness stopped when she realized that her words would bring no comfort to Sinbad.

The Skeleton, now broken from his trance, held the crystal out to Sinbad, "Here... I am finished... you need it now..." The Skeleton's voice had changed; the harsh tone was replaced by one of amazement and wonder. "I... know who I am now..."

Sinbad, still reeling from the shock of seeing Krassa dead, was oblivious to the Skeleton's words. But seeing the crystal in front of him, he had the sudden realization that if he wished the Sultan well again, things could still turn out in his favor! He raced towards the Skeleton, arms outstretched to take the crystal from him, when a tremendous force knocked Sinbad off his feet and he crashed to the ground. Lord Yar had struck the Gatekeeper such a tremendous blow that had sent the colossal raven-human colliding into Sinbad, pinning his legs to the floor with his considerable weight.

Sinbad struggled to free himself, but was forced to watch in horror as Lord Yar rounded on the Skeleton. The Skeleton had regained his senses, but it was too late. The Skeleton expertly thrust and stabbed at Lord Yar with his dagger, but the despot's armor absorbed every blow with ease. Lord Yar cut savagely at the Skeleton and managed to behead the warrior. Though he was not dead, the Skeleton could no longer see, and was feeling around on the ground for his severed head.

Pushing himself free from the Gatekeeper's limp body, Sinbad got to his feet and raised his sword in defiance, but his spirit dropped as soon as he saw the crystal gleaming in Lord Yar's metal palm.

"You would ruin me for this, Sinbad?" Lord Yar growled. In an instant, Lord Yar closed his fist around the crystal with all of his might. Sinbad's heart broke as he heard the gem being crushed into tiny shards.

Sinbad lost his composure and charged at Lord Yar. Their swords collided with tremendous force as Sinbad launched into his attack. He quickly surmised, based on Lord Yar's lumbering movements and obvious openings, that Lord Yar was a much weaker combatant. Sinbad struck Lord Yar's armor with all of his might, but his sword was unable to penetrate his magically reinforced armor. Sinbad wished that Tishimi could be by his side; her katana could have dispatched this despot with ease. Lord Yar was a haughty, arrogant man. There must have been something he overlooked. Then Sinbad spotted it!

Lord Yar threw all of his strength behind every attack, and it was to his great frustration that Sinbad kept darting away like a troublesome fly. "Stay there!" Lord Yar barked at his opponent, but Sinbad remained consistently out of his reach. Suddenly, Lord Yar saw a glint in Sinbad's eye. Lord Yar could tell that Sinbad had devised a plan and was angered that he could not guess the sailor's next move. Sinbad performed a shoulder roll past Lord Yar's peripheral vision and ended up next to Lord Yar's leg.

A sharp, agonizing pain erupted from his calf muscle, and Lord Yar could barely catch his breath! He crashed down on one knee and then realized with great horror why his attendant was trying to stop him: the attendant did not finish placing his armor on him! As he cursed himself for being a fool, Lord Yar felt Sinbad yank the sword from his bloody calf and then wrench his helmet from his head. Casting the piece of armor aside like it was garbage, Sinbad fixed his ice-cold eyes on Lord Yar's.

"You have doomed a great man to his death and slaughtered others for your amusement. This is the least I can do," Sinbad stated flatly.

Lord Yar did not have the energy to resist, the crippling pain in his leg had seen to that. Sinbad grabbed Lord Yar by the neck and waist of his armor and, with a mighty heave, threw him over the balcony! Lord Yar plummeted head first to the sand of the arena below. It would be the only time that Lord Yar had been on the battlefield that he had built.

Sinbad caught his breath as he watched Lord Yar's body hit the ground and flop awkwardly on the sand. A few of the more feral monsters that Lord Yar imprisoned began fighting over the body, attempting to remove the armor and feasting on what they could reach. Though Sinbad felt that this was fitting, he was distraught. His mission had been to save the Sultan, and he had failed. Lord Yar's death brought him no satisfaction.

"Sinbad! Sinbad!" the Skeleton said as he made his way over to the sailor. Sinbad noticed that while the Skeleton's face was immobile, he thought he detected signs of happiness, which were reflected in the bony creature's expression.

"What is it?" Sinbad asked.

"The crystal... it really does do whatever you want it to! It is incredible!" the Skeleton shrieked.

"*Was* incredible," Sinbad corrected the Skeleton. "Now it is nothing but shattered rocks."

"But Sinbad, I can help you! I asked the crystal who I was, and it told me! My memory has been completely restored!"

"'Tis good news, but how will this help me?" Sinbad asked in a defeated tone. Yet there was something in the Skeleton's voice that dared to give him hope.

The Sultan Nesuah was sitting upright in his bed; younger, vigorous, and healthy. Sinbad was wrapping up his narrative, and Nesuah was excited.

"And that is when the Skeleton told me that he used to be a powerful wizard himself! Krassa was jealous of him, since he was far greater than he. So he cursed the Skeleton with a memory hex and tormented him in the arena for his own sadistic amusement."

"And once I remembered who I was, I was able to use my skills to lift Krassa's curse from you, sire," the Skeleton said with a bow.

Nesuah looked over at the Skeleton, who was now clad in a luxurious robe, befitting his new position. In gratitude for his service, Nesuah had made the Skeleton his servant, and gave him the laboratory that once belonged to Krassa.

"What a fantastic tale! And perhaps my favorite... and I admit I enjoy being the center of attention. Truly it was a grand adventure, and I am deeply moved that you would undertake such an enormous feat for my well-being," Nesuah said as he rose from his bed and shook Sinbad's hand with a firm, sincere grip.

"It seems to have worked out for everyone," Sinbad said. "The former captives of Lord Yar and Krassa have all returned to their homelands and their people. The Guardian and Raveness have led their people to a distant island, away from men, where they only serve themselves."

"But I do confess that I find it awkward to address you as Skeleton or Sorcerer. Since your memory was restored, pray tell, what is your true name?" Nesuah asked Skeleton.

Waving away the idea, the Skeleton said "Well, I do remember my name... but I have become so accustomed to being addressed as "Skeleton" that I have decided to keep the name... I feel it adds an air of mystery."

Sinbad and Nesuah laughed. "I am afraid I must take my leave, Sultan, for my crew is in need of shore-leave, and I must supervise the rowdy lot," Sinbad said as he began to exit Nesuah's room.

"Come visit soon!" Nesuah yelled after Sinbad. "I look forward to hearing of your adventures! May there be many more!"

"There shall!" Sinbad promised as he closed the door behind him.

# The End

# A Love Letter to Ray Harryhausen

This story is nothing more than a love letter to Ray Harryhausen and his remarkable artistic achievements. Though I was born long after his films were in theaters, my father showed them to me on VHS as a child. I was amazed and vowed to make a stop motion film myself one day. I tried... and realized quickly that I was no competition to the late, great Ray Harryhasuen (and yes, Lord Yar is simply Ray spelled backwards... I struggle with creating character names).

The creatures I featured in the story were ones that I would have loved to have seen in a Sinbad movie (with the Skeleton being an obvious homage to The Seventh Voyage of Sinbad or Jason and the Argonauts). I could not resist having the Griffin in the battle with the Centaur, because I was always bitter about how the events unfolded in the Golden Voyage of Sinbad (my personal favorite). Yet, I did not want the crew featured in Airship 27's lineup to play second fiddle, so I attempted to weave them into the plot without it feeling forced. I found that I loved writing for Henri and Ralf, so if I write another Sinbad epic, I will certainly feature something with them.

There is something I find interesting about prison escape stories, perhaps it is the ingenuity in the manner of the characters escaping. To me, it is appealing to see a hero, with the odds against them, make a clever use of their environment to escape. I knew the creatures that I had in Sinbad's stable were going to be his aids (in addition to his crew), but I spent the longest time pondering how to get his crew to lend a hand without resorting to pure brute force. Suddenly, it came to me to have the Basilisk eat outside of the stable, which then lent itself to Sinbad's escape plan coming to fruition... and I worry that I considered this the most logical breakout plan when I wrote it.

The fight with the Golem was an important one personally. I find, as a writer, that I am my own worst enemy. Many times when I am coming up with a story, I put my characters in as dangerous a position as I can imagine... only to find that I have stacked the odds so impossibly against them that the average person would die/get killed/get eaten etc... I am tempted to give up, and think to make the opponent a little less fearsome and give them an obvious weakness for the hero to exploit. It is then that I realized that the hero (in this case, Sinbad) is remarkable for a reason. He or she can overcome any challenge, though they may be beaten and battered to a pulp in the process. I feel that it is important for all heroes, they need to be what we strive to be: somebody who can beat the impossible. This brings me back to the Golem. I had an opponent that was seemingly unbeatable, but with a tremendous mental effort, I found a way for Sinbad to achieve the impossible. All it required was time, and not compromising a good idea for convenience, because that would be the greatest disservice of all to the readers.

I look forward to fighting the same creative battle with my next adventure for Airship 27.

**ERIK FRANKLIN** - is a writer/actor/filmmaker based in Seattle. Recently graduating with honors from the Art Institute of Seattle in film production, he is the co-President of Franklin-Husser Entertainment LLC. He is working on two upcoming feature films for his company: A dinosaur action film "Revenge of the Lost" and the martial arts comedy "3 Morons Fighting Ninja". You can give the company page a "Like" at: https://www.facebook.com/pages/Franklin-Husser-Entertainment-LLC/290795021042906.

Drawn to pulp fiction through his love of history, literature, and Americana, he is grateful for Airship 27 Productions giving him the opportunity to write his first story. He looks forward to writing more adventures!

# NYMPH MANIA
## by Carson Demmans

The Blue Nymph was at anchor. There had been no wind for days and the crew was exhausted from rowing. Most of the men had been sent to their bunks by Sinbad to rest. Sinbad himself looked in vain at the sky, hoping to see some cloud movement that might mean wind was coming. His first mate, Omar, busied himself doing nothing in particular but saw no point looking to the sky for something that was invisible. The wind would come. It always did.

In the crow's nest, Haroun slept. With no wind, nothing dangerous would approach them, and he was experienced enough to wake up at the slightest hint of a breeze.

The only other person on deck was Tishimi. She was the only woman on board, and the fact that she refused to take on any duties did not make the men resent her any less. Women were considered a jinx at sea, but her willingness to do any of the services of a sailor, or servicing sailors, would have made her tolerable. However, she considered herself a warrior, and nothing more or less. In battle, her swordsmanship and blood lust made her a formidable ally of the men, but she refused to take part in any of the celebration that followed a battle.

If Tishimi slept at all, nobody on board knew when or where. She would disappear from sight at times, but the crew knew it was safer and more pleasurable to enjoy her absence then seek her presence. The one man on the Blue Nymph that she could tolerate was Sinbad himself, but his conduct at the last port they were in had made that tolerance at an all time low. So, she was alone, not talking, not moving, and simply staring out at the calm sea.

Her razor-sharp senses alerted her to motion at the water line of the ship. She looked down, and to her left the water was moving, but it wasn't a wave. It took the form of a water spout, almost like a whale spouting. Instead of going straight up, though, it curved onto the deck and took shape. The shape solidified into the form of a woman, dressed all in different shades of blue. She turned and looked casually at Tishimi, who saw that the strange visitor's skin was also blue.

"Demon!" screamed Tishimi. The blue woman looked at her curiously but showed no fear. The lack of response to her battle cry angered Tishimi.

"Demon!" the warrior woman yelled a second time, much louder than the first.

The blue woman had a puzzled expression on her face as she snapped her fingers and another water spout sprung up from the sea and deposited another shape on the deck. This time, it was a horrible monster, humanoid in shape but covered with thick armor-like scales and arms which ended in fins with deadly looking pointed spines. The beast opened its mouth, displaying a double row of pointed teeth, all of which pointed inwards like a shark's. If it bit anyone, it was likely that person was going to lose a limb.

Tishimi's surprise lasted less than a second. The creature stood between her and the blue woman, so it had to die before she could dispatch the blue woman. A minor inconvenience at worst.

"A demon," the blue woman mumbled to herself. "What a strange thing to ask for."

Omar, Sinbad and Haroun had heard Tishimi's cry and acted quickly to help her. The crew needed something resembling excitement after days of boredom. Haroun scampered down the rigging of the ship like the monkey he was often accused of being the son of, doing a front flip onto the deck, pulling his scimitar out in mid-air. He was showing off, but as long as he quickly entered the battle, nobody would criticize him for it.

Omar rang a bell to summon the crew and screamed orders so loudly that the he drowned out the bell. Once he heard the sound of the rest of the crew coming up, the brawny man pulled out his own sword and advanced.

Rolf the Viking was the first man to come up on deck. He was the largest and heaviest of the crew members, but when a good fight was happening he would run twice as fast as anyone else to join it. He screamed his battle cry as he lifted his battle axe above his head to deliver a mighty blow to the sea demon. His axe bounced off the impregnable scaled of the beast with such momentum that he was knocked flat on his back.

Haroun laughed as he saw the giant's misfortune. The wiry sailor swung for the creature's legs. The edge of his sword caught between two scales and he was unable to pull it loose. He hung on as long as he could until the creature flung him aside, the scimitar still harmlessly wedged in the protective armor.

Omar was a veteran of more fights than the rest of the crew combined. He reasoned that if the creature had the mouth of a shark than it could be fought like a shark. Tishimi was busy fighting her way through the demon's fearsome fins, so Omar approached the creature from the side and aimed the swing of his sword at the beast's eyes.

He was partially successful in the sense that he failed less than Rolf or Haroun. He struck close enough to an eye to cause the creature agony if not injury, and in return received both agony and injury as the demon backhanded him. The spines did not touch Omar, but the brute strength of the creature was enough to send him flying against a mast.

"Use your heads, men!" Omar yelled. "That thing's a sea demon if I ever saw one!"

Rolf sprung to his feet, lowered his head, and took a running start at the demon. He hit it with a thud that any goat would have envied, but the demon was unfazed.

"That doesn't work either!" Rolf yelled back and he picked up his ax again.

The rest of the crew was on deck now, but there wasn't enough room for all of them to attack one foe at once. They began advancing in waves, with a new group coming forward as the one before it was defeated.

Sinbad was still on an upper deck, watching the progress of the battle, looking for an opening. For the first time, he saw the blue woman, watching the battle from several feet away. He did not know if she was friend or foe, but he was willing to give her the benefit of the doubt. He swung on a rope toward her, planning on carrying her to safety. Instead, he felt like he had swung into a tree that he was unable to uproot, his arm uselessly wrapped around her trunk.

She looked down at him in amusement.

"Hello," she said sweetly. "Normally people greet me by bowing or shaking my hand. I think I like this better. How long is it customary for you to keep your arm wrapped around my waist?"

"I am trying to get you to safety!" Sinbad grunted, still trying to move the woman.

"How sweet. What am I in danger of?" she asked.

Sinbad looked at her with a blank expression on his face. Her eyes were reacting to light, so she wasn't blind, and had seen the demon fighting his entire crew. She was either insane or stupid, and either way she could be a threat herself.

"I was trying to get you away from that monster!" Sinbad exclaimed.

"Which one?" the blue woman asked innocently. "The lady in black or the giant who thinks he's a sheep? Then again, the monkey man looks a little shifty, too."

"The green thing with the teeth and the claws that's trying to kill everyone on board," Sinbad explained. The blue woman laughed in reply.

"Oh, that!" she said. "That's not a monster! That's a demon! It's a subtle distinction, I admit, but they are very sensitive about it. Call a monster a demon, and they'll never speak to you again. Call a demon a monster, and it will run off and sulk for days. Try it."

Sinbad looked at her in disbelief, but nothing else had worked, so it was worth a try.

"Monster!" Sinbad yelled. "You are nothing but a monster!"

The effect was magical. The demon froze in its tracks and looked at Sinbad with disgust. It tossed aside Tishimi and the men closest to it, discarded Haroun's sword, and dove over the railing of the ship into the water, never to be seen again.

"Who is the captain of this ship?" the blue woman asked.

Sinbad raised his hand suspiciously.

"Excellent!" the blue woman cried. "Then it is you who must have summoned me, just as I summoned that demon."

"You summoned that demon?" screamed Tishimi. "Why?"

"Because you asked me to," the blue woman said. "You distinctly said demon when I came on board, so out of common courtesy I got you one. You're welcome."

"Either she goes or I go!" Tishimi yelled in frustration. The blue woman snapped her fingers and a wave sprung up from the sea and dragged a screaming Tishimi away when it retreated back to the sea.

"What a strange girl," the blue woman said to nobody in particular. "When she gets what she asks for she gets even angrier.

Sinbad ran to the railing but Tishimi was already out of sight.

"Bring her back!" Sinbad yelled.

"Why?" the blue woman said. "Whenever I grant a wish around here it seems to make things worse."

"Bring her back and you shall have my gratitude forever!" Sinbad pledged.

The blue woman took him at his word and snapped her fingers. Another wave, sprung up and deposited a soaking wet Tishimi in a heap on the deck. She gasped for air, with her sword still clutched in one hand.

"So, if I am to have your gratitude," the blue woman said with a smile, "I would like it in the form of your arm around my waist again. It felt rather nice. I don't know if I want it there forever or not, but let's try it for a few years and see how it goes."

When he did not respond immediately, the blue woman signalled Sinbad to obey by sternly patting her own waist with a hand. Sinbad complied, and she looked at him with approval.

"Thank you captain," she said. "I appreciate your gratitude. Now then, why did you summon me?"

"I did not summon you," Sinbad said with a confused looked on his face. "I don't even know your name."

"My name is Thoe," she said. "But that is not how you summoned me. You named your ship after me, and in doing so, you summoned me."

"The ship is called the Blue Nymph," Sinbad said.

"Exactly," Thoe replied. "And since I am the only blue nymph in the world, it must refer to me. Technically, I'm a Nereid, which is a type of nymph, but the Blue Nereid isn't much of a name for a ship, is it? Too hard to pronounce."

"Sinbad named this ship the Blue Nymph years ago," Omar said as he tried to shake the cobwebs out of his head after being thrown against the mast. "Why are you only coming to us now for the first time?"

"As I said," Thoe explained, "I am the only blue nymph in the world. I've been busy. Ship launchings, animal sacrifices, personal appearances, birthday parties. That sort of thing."

There was a loud gasp, and the crew turned as one to see what caused it. It was Tishimi, pulling herself up to her feet. Her black silk clothing clung to her body tighter than her own skin. The men all looked away, although the lecherous Frenchman Henri was the last to turn. He lusted for all women, and the athletic Tishimi was no different, other than she would kill him herself rather than having her husband do it. If she had a husband.

"Not a bad way to go," Henri thought as he finally turned his head. Thoe alone stared at Tishimi as the warrior woman departed for whichever hidden nook served as her living space.

"I think she looks better that way," Thoe said. "Wet and in those clinging clothes. I will create a festival in my own honor. Women shall wear tight tops named after me and will be doused with water to display their beauty. The winner shall be grandly rewarded."

"Wet Thoe shirt contests?" Henri asked. He liked the concept but not the name. "You might want to shorten that a bit."

Thoe shifted her weight so she leaned into Sinbad slightly. He was amazed with her weight. She was slenderly built and as graceful as a wave but she was heavier than anyone on board.

"Besides," Thoe cooed sweetly," the name of your ship is not the only way you summoned me. Don't I look familiar? I was your inspiration."

Omar was regaining his faculties at an increasing rate and addressed Thoe directly.

"Look young lady," the middle-aged Omar said firmly but affectionately, "I was with Sinbad when he had this ship outfitted and named it. You did not come up at all. And if I haven't seen you before, I doubt he has either."

Thoe opened her eyes wide and stared directly into Omar's eyes. There was a second of realization in his eyes before salt water stung them. Thoe had summoned another wave, and this one had sucked the sturdy sailor off of the ship as easily as it had the light Tishimi.

In seconds, Omar found himself riding the top of a water spout directly in front of the Blue Nymph. He was staring slack jawed at the figure carved into the prow of the ship. Two bright blue gems stared at him from the eye sockets of the wood carving. Then salt water stung his eyes again as he was sucked back underwater and deposited back on deck where he had stood before. His clothes clung to him.

"Yes," Thoe said thoughtfully. "I think my festivals will be for female contestants only."

"The mermaid!" Omar gasped. "The blue woman's face and eyes look exactly like the mermaid carved on the prow!"

"Actually, I came first, so she looks like me," Thoe corrected Omar. "That is why I must have been your inspiration. I am not fond of the fish body and tail, but some artistic license must be allowed, I suppose. Who decided what the mermaid would look like?"

"I did," Sinbad admitted. "I sketched it for the wood carvers and then supervised all of the carving. I put the jewels that are her eyes in the settings myself."

"Well done," Thoe congratulated him. "The eyes are my favorite part. So having established beyond a doubt that you summoned me, why did you do it?"

"I don't know," Sinbad said, desperately straining his memory as what his inspiration for the name of his ship and the appearance of its mascot had been.

"Well, when you think of it, at least I'll be close by to hear it," Thoe said as she pulled his arm tighter around her waist. She began walking and Sinbad had no choice but to follow, her superior mass pulling him along.

"You have much to be grateful for," Thoe said admiringly as she inspected the Blue Nymph. "I inspired you to build an amazing vessel. I have never set foot on a ship before because none of them looked interesting. This one however is truly beautiful."

"It is a working ship," Sinbad said, "not a show piece. If it looks pleasing it is because it is so well constructed. The wood is strong and the shape is sleek."

"Well constructed and sleek," Henri said admiringly as he watched Thoe from behind. "She was definitely his inspiration."

The Frenchman had not meant her to hear the comment, but when she looked back at him over her shoulder, he attempted to apologize.

"I did not mean to offend you," Henri offered.

"You didn't offend me," Thoe replied. "If you had, I would have done this."

A wave sucked Henri offboard and then a water spout threw him high in the air. He landed roughly on the ship's deck, only to be swept off by a second wave and then thrown high up into the ship's riggings by a second water spout.

"Do you see the difference now?" Thoe asked helpfully. She walked on, dragging Sinbad with her. He was trying to be cautious. Whatever this woman was; powerful was one of the best adjectives to describe her.

"Haroun," Sinbad said as he gestured with his free hand at Henri. The agile sailor scampered up to the Frenchman and helped free him.

Rafi, the self-appointed ship's doctor approached Thoe and Sinbad. He was the oldest member of the ship's crew and the best educated in all matters Greek.

"I know something about nymphs," he said politely. "Sometimes you help sailors and sometimes you torment them with pranks or tortures."

"Yes," Thoe admitted. "Because some sailors are nice and some are complete idiots who deserve to be ripped apart by sharks."

"That is your idea of torture?" Rafi asked.

"No, a prank," Thoe said. "Torture is far worse."

Sinbad was losing his patience with the strange woman.

"You speak in riddles and want us to be your friend while you intimidate and threaten us!" he accused waving both of his arms around for emphasis. His pleading ended with him standing in front of her, both palms open, begging.

"What do you want?" Sinbad asked.

"Your ship," Thoe sighed. "You took your arm off of my waist. Your ship isn't as nice a show of gratitude, but now it will have to do."

"You can't take my ship!" Sinbad shouted.

"Of course, I can," Thoe replied. "I could also rip it apart with a slight wave of my hand, or create a giant whirlpool which would lay it on the sea floor for all eternity with all hands aboard. But, I like it and I like you. Every ship needs a captain so you will stay aboard at my pleasure. Quite possibly for my pleasure as well. I am not sure about your crew, however. They will need to be tested to prove their worth."

With that comment the water near the Blue Nymph boiled. A huge column rose up from the water, but it was of flesh, not fluid. The column coiled and the thing that was where a head should have been turned towards the ship. The top of the column opened revealing rows and rows of teeth reaching as far into the creature as they could see. All members of the crew were paralyzed with shock except one.

"Oh, so you have those here too," William Byrne, the lone Scotsman on board, said. "I had always wondered about that."

"Do you know this beast?" Sinbad asked.

"Not personally," William replied. "That's why I'm still alive. But, they are found in the land I come from. I have heard many stories about them."

"Do you know how to kill it?" Omar asked.

"No," William admitted. "But if it's any comfort to you, nobody else has ever figured that out either."

"Is there any way we can drive it off if we can't kill it?" Sinbad asked.

"Sure," William said. "Feed it until it's full and it will go away on its own!"

"Demon!" Sinbad yelled. The creature did not respond.

"Monster!" Sinbad screamed in desperation.

"Nice try," Thoe smirked. "But I deliberately chose a creature with no ears. You can call it whatever you want and it won't hear you."

"I think we're in trouble," Rolf said. It was unusual for the Norseman to be anything but overjoyed in battle, but now he seemed glum. "Do you remember the stories I told you about the great sea beast of the north? The Kraken?"

Sinbad nodded.

"I think I can see pieces of one stuck between this monster's teeth!"

Tishimi came back up onto deck wearing a dry set of silks. She held her long sword in one hand and her dagger in the other.

"My katana can cut through anything magical and kill it!" she snarled.

"Yes, the Frenchman told me that while he was looking down my dress," Thoe said. "He said many other things too, but that was the only thing of interest. That's why I chose a beast that is not magical. There are just as many natural monsters as there are supernatural ones."

"Raise anchor!" Sinbad commanded.

"There is no wind!" Omar complained.

"But there are waves!" Sinbad yelled. "The ship is bobbing like a cork! We can use the creature's own wake against it."

The monster had not moved much other than twitching. It had no eyes, ears or nose, and little brain to speak of. It had a dim awareness that it was not where it was supposed to be. The water was warmer than the deep lochs it favored and it was disoriented.

The giant Rolf was strong enough to reel the anchor in on his own, but as many crew members as could fit helped him raise the anchor in record time. The ship was driven away from the creature as it made waves with each movement of its body.

Touch was the one sense that the creature did have, and it was quite sensitive. As the Blue Nymph moved with the waves, it caused disturbances of its own. The creature struck, but missed. The ship was partially swamped by the waves it created. The creature began to rise again for another strike.

"Tishimi," William said in a plaintive tone," I don't do this out of any spite but only because you are the bravest person I have ever seen or known."

With that the Scotsman hurled the Japanese woman overboard. The disturbance caused by her caught the beast's attention. William made the sign of the cross with his hands.

"You will go no further and won't touch the woman!" William commanded. "Go back at once!"

"What are you doing?" Omar snapped. "Hoping the thing will choke on her swords?"

"There is a legend that St. Columba drove off the creature by calling on his God. Mind you the same legend says he could draw water from a rock, but I thought it was worth a try."

"A saint?" Sinbad asked. "A holy man?"

"Something like that," William said. "I am not a holy man myself, but it's the only other thing I know about it."

"You don't believe," Sinbad screamed. "But I believe in my god. Allah! Hear me? Save us!"

"Allah!" Omar yelled. "I have cursed you many times but I never will again! Save us!"

"Odin!" Rolf added. "Kill this beast! I am ready to go to Valhalla but my friends are not!"

Henri began praying in French and Haroun named every god he had ever heard of in his travels. The beast showed no response.

"Can you not defend yourself and your crew?" Thoe asked. Sinbad turned on her angrily.

"No!" he yelled. "But you can! You brought it here! You can send it away! I don't know if you are a goddess or a demi-god or a madwoman! But you can save us! Do you want me to beg! I'll beg! Do you want me to be grateful for life? I will! Take my life and save my crew! You claim ownership of my boat! Save it for yourself!"

Rafi stepped forward and said something in Greek. It was poorly pronounced but Thoe nodded. The creature sank down into the depths and found itself back in its home shortly thereafter.

"Your doctor says that you would give me anything that I wanted to save your crew including your own life. What I wanted was a noble man with a loyal crew. I have that now. That is what I wanted."

"Tishimi!" Rolf yelled.

"No," Thoe added. "I really don't want her. Thanks for asking, though."

"We need to save her!" Henri yelled. His motive was partially chivalrous and mainly motivated by wanting to see her in wet silks again.

"She will already be dead," Thoe said.

"No!" William said. "I chose her because that woman's life is nailed to her

"ALLAH! HEAR ME? SAVE US!"

spine! That beastie couldn't kill her more than anything else could!"

"I see her!" Henri yelled. The Frenchman had the sharpest eyes on the ship. He pointed her out to Sinbad, who tied a long rope to himself. He had the Frenchman point the spot to the Viking and Rolf launched his captain as far as he could. Sinbad swam towards Tishimi, but the warrior woman had been knocked unconscious. It was a struggle for Sinbad to swim dragging the rope behind him but he finally reached Tishimi and tied the rope around her. He then hung onto the rope with all of his life. Without having given the order he knew that Henri would be keeping close watch on him and signal to Rolf begin hauling in the rope. No other member of the crew would be able to match the giant Norseman's fury in hauling in his captain and shipmate. The Viking would exert himself until he died if necessary, knowing that his dream of going to Valhalla would finally happen.

Rolf was exhausted but proud when he finally hauled Sinbad and Tishimi on deck. Rafi rushed to Tishimi and began working to revive her.

Sinbad looked at Thoe with disdain. She only smiled in reply.

"Congratulations," she said. "You and your crew passed the test."

Sinbad gritted his teeth before he answered.

"I suspected as much," he growled. "Only you could save us from that monster and you did so rather than let us be killed by it. You could have saved Tishimi just as easily but you refused. What would you have done if we did not rush to save her? Let her die?"

"Oh no!" Thoe replied. "That would have been cruel! I would have summoned another water demon to eat her alive! That would be a far more fitting end for her. She seems to like demons for some reason."

By now Tishimi had regained consciousness.

"Where is William?" She said as loudly as she could while still exhaling sea water.

The Scotsman stepped toward her.

"You did that knowing I would suvive and was likely to gut you like a fish?"

"True," he said. "But I was also trying to save everyone else on this ship."

William knew that he couldn't survive a fight with Tishimi. At best, he'd fatally wound her while she killed him. She pulled herself up, nodded to the Scotsman and wandered off to wherever her hidden sanctum was. Thoe remained standing still, smiling at Sinbad. She would continue to hold that pose long after he and his crew had left her, convincing everyone of her power and her insanity, and making them wonder which was greater.

"Pirates!" Haroun bellowed from his crow's nest.

The wind had begun blowing since early that morning and the Blue Nymph had been able to sail for a few hours. It was approaching land and had crossed paths with the scavengers who patrolled near shores, knowing that eventually all ships have to go ashore.

Sinbad ran to find Thoe and found her standing immobile where he had left her the previous day. She smiled as he ran to her.

"Is this your doing?" he yelled at her. "The pirates?"

"No," she said pleasantly. "Would you like me to destroy them for you?"

"If you want to do anything, don't move or lift a finger in any way!" Sinbad said sternly. "I can't trust you. I and my crew have fought pirates many times and we have always triumphed. Just don't do anything to hinder us."

Thoe tilted her head as she looked at Sinbad with curiosity. He was a very proud man, but had been willing to sacrifice his pride the day before when he begged her for her help. She had actually been telling the truth about having not summoned the pirates or her ability to destroy them easily, and she suspected that he knew that. Mortals often acted strangely around mythical beings such as herself but she had never met anyone quite like the legendary sailor.

"We could turn and run," Omar suggested. "The men are still tired from rowing for days, Tishimi is not recovered, and we have no cargo to protect. What do you think Sinbad?"

Sinbad did not reply to his first mate immediately. Instead, Omar only heard the sound of metal on metal. Omar turned to make sure that his captain was still behind him.

"I'm sorry, Omar," Sinbad apologized. "I was just sharpening my sword. Are you ready for battle, old friend?"

Omar glared at Sinbad, who only laughed.

"I heard every word you said, Omar. I always do," Sinbad said. "But, we rely on our reputation as the fiercest ship on the seas. If we face this attack, the next five will retreat when they see our sail. Besides, even if I listened to you, do you think they would?"

Sinbad gestured at his crew. Rolf was twirling his ten-pound ax as if it were a toy. Henri was practicing fencing moves. Haroun stood with a scimitar in each hand. William stood in front of all of them. Sinbad was curious about that as the Scotsman was fierce in battle but never the first to rush into it. He understood when she saw Tishimi trying to muscle her way through her shipmates to get to the front of the small army.

"Use me as your shield, girl!" William barked at the warrior woman. "It's the least I owe you. You aren't at full strength and I'm to blame for that."

Tishimi took a step back and then threw herself onto the deck of the ship. Her silk garments allowed her to slide between William's legs before he realized what was happening. She looked back at him with an expression that was as close as she ever came to smiling.

"You trusted me to help save the ship yesterday," Tishimi growled. "Trust me to do the same again today."

'And do we have a plan for this battle?" Omar asked Sinbad sarcastically.

"There are three pirate ships ahead," Sinbad explained. "I have Rafi at the wheel. He is to aim for the middle ship but then veer to the right. The Blue Nymph is far more maneuverable than any of them. We'll engage the outermost ship and be gone before the other two ships can react."

"Thank you," Thoe said. Sinbad was startled. She had moved up beside him silently and was listening to his every word. "I can move very well, but it's nice of you to notice."

Sinbad ignored her. He looked up to Rafi, who was not a sailor by trade but who had learned to be one out of necessity. The rest of the crew would leap overboard at the slightest provocation for battle and leave the ship unattended if they had their way.

"There is a reason these maniacs hired me as ship's doctor as their first crew member," he mused. He looked down at Thoe. He had lied to Sinbad about the contents of his conversation in Greek with her. Like Sinbad, there was little he wouldn't do to save the ship and its crew. He had spoken out of desperation to Thoe and without permission to do so. He only hoped he would be able to explain his actions when the time came. At the signal from Sinbad, he steered the ship and brought it alongside the outermost of the pirate ships.

The crew of the Blue Nymph boarded the pirate ship with such zeal that the pirates were taken aback. There were many tales of the blood lust of the Blue Nymph's crew, so many in fact that most pirates assumed they were exaggerations.

In reality, they were gross understatements.

Haroun was the first to set foot on the enemy ship, swinging wildly on a rope he held with one hand, with a scimitar in his other hand and another in his belt. Tishimi found herself pulled back roughly as William surged ahead of her, swinging wildly. Tishimi grimaced. The tough Scotsman was trying to protect her and she resented it. The only reason she did not strike him down herself was that Rafi had relayed the comment about her life being nailed to her spine, and she took it as a compliment. Sinbad struck a pose on the railing of his ship, and hailed the pirate ship.

"Surrender!" he yelled. "You tried to lay a trap on us but we have sprung it on you!"

"I know who you are, Sinbad," the grizzled pirate captain laughed. "And you are right; we were lying in wait for you. If you had paid more attention, you might have realized the nature of our trap."

Pirates of the other two ships were swarming from their ships onto the one that Sinbad had boarded. The pirates had rigged ropes and planks so that with some effort the crews of all three could face any ship foolhardy enough to board one of them.

"I take it that I have used this strategy once too often," Sinbad said ruefully.

"Once was too often indeed!" Omar snapped. "Our entire crew is already in battle so we have no choice but to try and win this battle."

Sinbad grinned as he leaped to the enemy ship. He was a sailor first and foremost, but adventure was part and parcel of his life on the sea. The crews of the other two ships were trying to outflank his crew, but the limited space of the pirate ship that had been boarded limited their effectiveness. Sinbad had not even drawn his scimitar yet. He was throwing pirates over the rail and into the sea. He laughed at his own cleverness as Omar grimaced. Sinbad was his best friend but at times he fell into the role of surrogate father for the younger man.

In the heart of the battle, Rolf was swinging his ax with wild abandon. His crewmates had learned to duck his blows and throw enemies into his path. The Viking screamed his incoherent battle cry at the top of his lungs. It contained no words, but was his signal to the Valkyries that he was ready to be taken by them upon his death.

Tishimi was a blur of steel and silk. She demonstrated more skill and finesse in ten seconds than Rolf had in his entire life. What she lacked in brute strength she made up for with expertly placed razor-sharp blades.

If Sinbad had posed, Henri absolutely pranced. The Frenchman was a spectacle as he leaped and feinted, delighting himself and puzzling his opponents. William had learned long before that the Frenchman made an excellent distraction that he could use to his advantage.

Haroun had made his way over the battle to the other pirate ships and set them free. They had foolishly been left unattended and he screamed out his success. The pirates realized their folly and scrambled to recover their other two ships. Sinbad laughed as he lifted his sword to signal victory. In doing so, he made himself a target for the grizzled pirate captain. The older man was no swordsman, but could still throw a knife better than most. He drew back his arm and let his blade fly, piercing Sinbad's heart.

There was an inhuman scream that made all pirates and sailors look back in terror. Thoe flowed rather than leapt as she appeared on the pirate ship. Waves grabbed pirates as if the water was alive and threw pirates into the sea where sharks now swarmed at the nymph's command. She picked up Sinbad as if he was weightless and moved like a wave as she returned to the Blue Nymph.

"Doctor!" she screamed. Rafi was already in motion but he lost all hope as he saw the wound.

"I cannot save him," he said sadly. Thoe was undeterred.

"Just keep him alive, old man!" she commanded. "Let me do the rest!"

Rafi applied pressure to the wound and suddenly found himself riding on top of a wave. Somehow he could stand on it as if it were solid ground. Thoe's face was grim determination as she made the water carry her and the two men at lightning speed. They reached a small island where an altar stood.

"Panacea!" Thoe screamed. "I beg of you!"

The Greek goddess of universal remedy appeared out of curiosity rather than duty. She knew Thoe but had little use for her or any other nymph. They were more like forces of nature than a god who served a specific purpose.

"Heal him!" Thoe demanded. Panacea shrugged.

"You are no friend of mine, and you are no god," Panacea said. "Why should I?"

"She is a god," Rafi lied. "She has a temple in her name! It is the ship I sail on, the Blue Nymph!"

"A ship as a temple?" Panacea mused. "And do you worship her?"

"I will if she can prompt you to do a miracle!" Rafi said. Sinbad was at death's door.

Panacea laughed. In truth she had been flattered that she had been called on rather than her father, the god of medicine. She drew a dagger and cut herself. Her blood flowed into Sinbad's wound, and both her cut and his wound healed simultaneously.

"Keep your word, healer!" Panacea warned Rafi as she disappeared. "What I can cure I can inflict as well!"

Rafi dropped to his knees in front of Thoe.

"You are a goddess," he said sincerely.

Thoe said nothing. Sinbad was reviving and she led the confused sailor and Rafi to the edge of the island and summoned another wave which took all of them back to the Blue Nymph.

The crew was astounded as a living Sinbad rejoined them. He was still groggy from massive blood loss and winced as Omar hugged him. Tishimi nodded at Thoe. In her own way the nymph had proven herself in battle and saved Sinbad. It was enough to make the blue woman tolerable, for the time being at least. Rafi told his tale to the slack jawed crew members. Sinbad was the most shocked of all.

"I owe you everything," Sinbad said to Thoe. "Rafi is right. You are a goddess."

"You are the captain of a ship I am proud to own and my betrothed," Thoe said with great affection. "What else could I do?"

"Sinbad, may I speak to you?" Rafi said as he tugged on his captain's arm.

"I think you should," Sinbad growled as he followed the healer. Thoe was enjoying the adulation she was receiving and did not notice.

"I did not quite give you the full account of what I told Thoe when the monster attacked," Rafi admitted.

"Then give me a full account now, Rafi, or I swear that an entire ship full of goddesses can't save you!"

"I know a little about nymphs and their kin," Rafi said. "They verge on being goddesses but fall short in many ways. I played to her need of being seen as a mighty being. I said that you could only love a blue nymph and no other and would pledge the remainder of your life to such. I meant the ship, not her, but did not clarify."

"We were all trying to save the ship and crew, Rafi," Sinbad conceded. "But is there any reason you pledged my life and not your own?"

"Thoe looks at you as if you were a god and she were a mere mortal, captain," Rafi said. "I will do my best now to reason with her, I am not sure that reason is something she appreciates."

"Thoe," Rafi said as he approached the nymph and an astonished crew.

"Your betrothed was explaining her plans for your honeymoon, Sinbad," Omar chuckled. "Exactly how long can you hold your breath?"

"Thoe," Rafi repeated. "As the priest of your floating temple, I want to speak about your upcoming wedding with my captain. Are you familiar with his religion?"

The nymph shook her head.

"He is allowed to have many wives," Rafi said slyly. "Are you prepared to share him?"

"Have you ever seen what happens to ripples in a pond when pebbles are thrown in?" Thoe mused. "They multiply."

Thoe shimmered and her form rippled. Soon there were half a dozen replicas of Thoe on deck.

"I can create them out of sea mist," Thoe explained. "I can make as many as are needed and make them disappear with a mere blink."

"And if Sinbad doesn't need all of them, could other arrangements be made?" Henri said hopefully.

"And then there is a matter of a dowry," Rafi said, his mind racing.

"A dowry?" Thoe asked. "Will gold do?"

She did not wait for an answer. A water spout formed beside the ship and deposited a stream of gold coins on the deck.

"There are tons of these on the sea floor, left by sunken ships," Thoe explained. "I would be glad to cleanse the sea of them."

"Life is not easy on a ship," Rafi continued. "Unlike you, we require food and water, things beyond your needs."

Thoe shrugged. She gestured and a stream of water filled an empty barrel.

"That is salt water," Rafi said. "We can not drink it.

Thoe smiled and salt appeared on the deck beside the barrel.

"The water is fresh now, priest," Thoe said. "I can give you all that you need."

"This is fine salt," Omar said as he inspected it. "A ship can always use salt, for cooking, cleansing wounds, preserving fish. And you can make it whenever you want?"

Thoe nodded.

"And what would the captain's lady like for a wedding present?" Omar asked politely. "It seems you can provide for this ship better than Sinbad ever could."

With another wave of her hand, a wave of fish landed on the deck.

"I can bring you fish from all over the world," Thoe said. "You'll never want for food."

"Cod!" Rolf said happily. "Thank you Mrs. Sinbad!"

Tishimi picked up a rare Japanese puffer fish.

"A delicacy," she admitted. "But, these men think having women on board is bad luck."

Thoe jumped over the ship railing, only to be buoyed up by one of the waterspouts she commanded.

"I can step off the ship whenever anyone desires," Thoe said.

"Wind," Tishimi said, wanting to remain the sole female on board.

"If you have it, please move away from me," Thoe said. "I have a very sensitive nose."

"No," Sinbad said quickly. "I know what she means. You said you could provide us with anything we need. You can't provide us with wind. The air is beyond your control."

"True," Thoe sighed. "But wind is nothing more than a current of air, and there are many kinds of currents."

The Blue Nymph began moving, pushed by waves and moving against the wind.

"As I was saying," Omar said, "is there anything in particular you would like as a wedding gift?"

"This ship will do," Thoe said. "Your healer has proclaimed it as my temple, so I have a greater claim to it than before."

"Is there anything else your priest promised you?" Sinbad said. His crew was becoming quite enamored with the idea of him marrying this creature.

"Children," Thoe said.

"I hope he fathers many with you," Sinbad grumbled. Thoe laughed.

"You do not fool me, Sinbad," Thoe said. "You test my love for you as I tested your worthiness. You created a mighty ship in my name. Let me make it even mightier with our union."

"You always said you would do anything for this ship and your crew," Omar whispered to Sinbad. "She saved your life, Sinbad, She can make you rich and powerful, and protect this crew like no other. I have had six wives, and all of them combined could not offer what she does."

Sinbad looked at the beautiful nymph. She was a spitting image of his ship's mascot, and seemed to have some uncanny connection to the ship, but what was it? As Sinbad pondered this problem, the sea boiled. A giant figure rose from the sea. But, it was simply not rising. It was absorbing sea water and expanding in size. It was roughly the shape of a man, but was constantly changing in shape.

"Demon? Sinbad asked Thoe. "Monster?"

"Far worse," Thoe said angrily. "It's my ex."

"I am power!" the water creature shrieked. "I am eternal! I am a god!"

"You are annoying," Thoe said, mocking his regal tone. "Hello, Proteus. What do you want?"

"For you to be my bride!" Proteus exclaimed.

"And by bride, you mean step-mother to the monstrous children you fathered with your sister? Raising a bunch of inbred freaks that sea demons call ugly? Let me think for a second. No, I'm good. Goodbye, Proteus."

"You cannot leave me!" Proteus screamed. As he grew angry a storm began to brew.

"I can and I did. I left you a note," Thoe said. "I returned your ring and moved out. This ship is my home now, my temple, and will one day be where I raise my own children with the captain of this ship, Sinbad. He built it in my name and with my image. You can't even remember by birthday!"

"I remembered it!" Proteus said. "I was just a day late."

"Fascinating," Thoe said. "We'll send you a wedding invitation, but feel free to just send a gift instead of coming."

The shape of the water being began to become more defined. Proteus was

"SHE CAN MAKE YOU RICH AND POWERFUL."

a handsome man now, a hundred feet tall from his waistline at the water and rising up to a handsome bearded face. Other than his gigantic size, he could have passed for a relative of Sinbad.

"Oh no you don't" Thoe said sternly. "I'm not falling for your shape shifting tricks again. The last time we broke up you tried to hookup with me in a different identity. Sinbad is a mortal, Proteus, and not some demigod you can impersonate."

Proteus began to shrink until he was no more than six feet in height, his extra mass dispersed as mist. A water spout similar to the ones that Thoe favored carried him up onto deck.

"My skills have improved since you last saw me," Proteus bragged.

"Not the skills I wanted you to learn," Thoe snapped. "Your sister has lower standards in that department than I do. Ask anyone."

Sinbad laughed. Proteus became even angrier.

"Do not tempt me, mortal!" Proteus snarled. "I could crush you and your ship in a split second!"

"My ship," Thoe corrected. "I own it and Sinbad is its captain."

Proteus pointed at Sinbad and laughed.

"You take orders from a mere female!" Proteus snorted.

"At least I have a female to take orders from!" Sinbad replied. His crew laughed. Thoe allowed herself a slight giggle and looked at Sinbad approvingly. "The sea is full of sirens, mermaids and other creatures. Many human women would love to have a god for a husband, especially shape shifters. Take the form of a swan. I am told that is a popular choice."

"Do not presume to speak to me, mortal!" Proteus said. He took a step forward and Tishimi struck him with her sword. He winced. The blade went through him like it was passing through water and he did not bleed, but he was clearly wounded.

"Interesting," Thoe said. 'If you were truly a god as you always claimed, that wouldn't hurt you. You're a magical being, not much different from me. You're a cheat, a liar, and you smell funny. Go away Proteus."

"You do not order me, woman!" Proteus said. "I command you! You are mine!"

"Tishimi!" Sinbad yelled. The warrior woman took the cue and struck Proteus once more.

"Stop doing that!" Proteus yelled. "What kind of captain are you that allows women on your ship? Are there not enough whores in ports to satisfy you?"

Tishimi prepared to strike Proteus again and Sinbad waved her off.

"Tishimi is one of the finest warriors I have ever seen and a valued member of my crew. Thoe is capable of miracles. Something made me name this ship after her and put her likeness on its prow. Maybe she and I are destined to be together. In any event, you and she are not. I order you off my ship."

Sinbad paused.

"I mean our ship," he said. Thoe nodded in approval. Proteus spat in disgust.

"You hide behind women," Proteus mocked. "You are not a man at all. Your witch can hurt me with her magic sword, but you can do nothing to me."

To the amazement of everyone, Tishimi tossed her katana to Sinbad. He swung it experimentally, admiring its balance.

"I am a samurai, not a witch," Tishimi said. "I am also a member of this crew and no man's whore. Whatever type of being this blue woman is, she does not belong to you."

Proteus gestured and chains appeared on Thoe's wrists, forming out of the sea mist that had been part of his giant form. Sinbad cut the chains effortlessly with the katana.

"I could get used to this," Sinbad said, admiring the sword.

"Don't," Tishimi corrected. She was begrudgingly trying to help get rid of the repulsive water man, but she had her limits.

"Fight me in your human form," Sinbad challenged.

"I have no sword," Proteus said. He soon had half a dozen of them thrown at his feet by various crew members. He reluctantly picked one up and faced Sinbad.

The sailor was on the sea deity in a second, the katana slicing into Proteus's arms half a dozen times. Proteus grimaced. He swung wildly. He connected once with the katana out of pure luck, and Sinbad was amazed at his strength. Sinbad was knocked down to one knee by the force of the blow. Proteus moved in for the kill. Sinbad took the opportunity to thrust the katana completely through the water man's torso.

Proteus was in agony, but managed to pull the katana out of himself. Tishimi quickly recovered her enchanted blade. He looked at Sinbad with pure hatred. He dove over the ship's railing and disappeared into the sea, only to reappear as an entire army of water monsters that surrounded the ship.

"She is my property! I own her!" Proteus yelled. "She is my slave!"

"You can't own her any more than anyone can own the oceans or the skies, Proteus!" Sinbad yelled. 'You are a fool! If you were the greatest god of them all, she would still be too good for you!"

"I will destroy you and your entire crew!" Proteus shouted. "I will dissolve her into sea foam and only return her to this form when my lust requires it!"

"You are a coward!" Sinbad accused. "A common tyrant who deserves to die alone!"

The sky darkened, but it was actually the gigantic form of a woman coming between the sun and the ship. Sinbad looked at the face of the gigantic woman, and it was the most beautiful woman he had ever seen.

"Aphrodite?" Thoe gasped.

The sky filled with the forms of Greek goddesses and angels. An entire squadron of armored women riding winged horses attacked from the north.

"Valkyries!" Rolf gasped.

The Valkyries were the smallest in stature but the first to attack Proteus. Aphrodite followed with a mighty blow from her giant hand. She dispersed a large portion of Proteus's form, driving it back into the sea. A dozen other deities followed suit.

When Proteus was dispersed, Panacea appeared on the ship in front of Rafi.

"I wouldn't be much of a doctor if I didn't check up on my patient."

The goddess turned to Sinbad.

"Live up to your words, human, and treat this nymph with the respect you say Proteus did not give her. Your words pleased the women of the religions of your crew. Do not disappoint us, or you will feel our wrath."

"Actually, the guy was a jerk, and I've been trying to get them to do this for years," Panacea whispered to Thoe. "You've traded up nymph. If you don't keep this one, I know half a dozen goddesses who will take him off your hands. The girls on the winged horses are interested too, but they scare even me."

The sky cleared and the deities faded from sight. Sinbad turned to Thoe.

"I have not always treated women with the respect that I have just said that you deserved," Sinbad confessed. There were several loud guffaws from his crew.

"Okay, so I've never done it," Sinbad admitted. "But, you are my superior in every way and a worthy master for this ship. If you will have me, Thoe, let me make you my wife."

"Silverware," Thoe said happily to Omar. "I would like silverware as a wedding gift."

Omar nodded in approval. He had married for far more impure motives, and on more than one occasion. The remaining men onboard did not have the same high opinion of women that Sinbad had just claimed to have, and they doubted his sincerity. However, they loved their captain more than life itself, and would never say anything against his wishes.

Tishimi stared at her katana. If it could harm Proteus, it could do the same to Thoe.

Strangely, she had no urge to do so. Sinbad had always treated her as an equal, and sometimes as his superior in some matters. He gave her free rein on the ship and in battle. He might honestly do the same with the nymph and live up to the hopes of the gods.

She made a mental note to pay Omar a portion of anything he spent on a gift of silverware.

In the days that followed, Thoe was usually found with Sinbad's arm firmly around her waist. She was always the one that put it there, but he had grown to enjoy it. Thoe had no interest in kissing, and sex was only mentioned in passing as part of their honeymoon. Sinbad did note that her body was not as dense as it was when he first met her. He assumed she had some sort of shape shifting power like Proteus.

When not with Sinbad, Thoe was often found on deck, staring at the sea. Tishimi did that often as well, so it was inevitable that they were regularly in close proximity to each other. Tishimi also assumed that Thoe had some control over her appearance. At times it was a light blue and on other days much darker.

One morning, Tishimi found Thoe bent over the railing, staring at some detail in the water below. The nymph often looked lost in thought, although Tishimi suspected she was actually lost with an absence of thought. The warrior woman rushed the nymph at full speed and dumped the blue woman overboard. Haroun saw the entire spectacle and was at a loss for words. Thoe could not be seen, and he suspected the worst. Tishimi seemed to have some sort of immunity to magic that he did not understand. The wiry sailor was not one of the great intellects of his time. He could not fathom the actions of ordinary women, let alone a samurai from a country he had never seen or a god-like blue woman. Finally, he did what he would have done if an ordinary woman had been thrown overboard.

"Man overboard! No! Woman overboard! No! Nymph overboard!" he screamed. A group of sailors congregated around Tishimi, who was smirking as she looked downwards. Omar tried to assess the situation.

"Did you kill her?" the first mate asked.

"No," Tishimi replied.

"Did you harm her in any way?" Omar continued.

"No," Tishimi said.

"I am not going to continue guessing, Tishimi!" Omar roared. "I know you don't think of yourself as a sailor, but you are still on this ship and subject to its rules! I am first mate! You will respect my authority!"

Tishimi stared blankly as the powerfully built, squat man. She did not respect his authority or that of any man over her. Still, she had seen Omar in battle and the many scars he had received. That she respected.

"I gave her a dunking," Tishiimi admitted. "She has done it to me enough times that I owed her a payback of some kind. Whatever she is, she is more at home in water than anywhere else. She'll be fine."

"And by fine do you mean gone forever?" Omar asked. Tishimi shrugged. The thought process of the nymph was beyond her, if it existed at all. She doubted that she had killed Thoe, but had no idea if the blue woman would return on her own accord.

"I know that you respect Sinbad if nobody else on this ship," Omar said curtly. "He feels something for Thoe, although I doubt even he knows what it is. If the two of them have anything in common, it is that logic is a foreign language they both refuse to learn. My thoughts are about the welfare of this ship, and Thoe can help ensure that. If nothing else, do not lie to me and say you have not enjoyed the extra salt you put on that poisonous blowfish you insisted on tempting death with the other day."

Tishimi listened to Omar but was not moved by anything he said. She agreed that Thoe had brought extra luxuries that Tishimi had greatly enjoyed, but luxuries meant little to her. She had been trained by her father in the ways of the Japanese army to survive at all costs. When necessary, she could live on next to no food or water and sleep in the open regardless of the elements, which she had been doing before she had first met Sinbad in Baghdad. She was not fond of life aboard the ship, but she was actually fonder of the crew than she would ever admit. She looked casually over one shoulder and saw that William was standing watch over, desperately trying to make up for throwing her to the loch monster. He did not realize that she would have dove into the water herself if she thought it would have helped the battle.

A blur ran by Tishimi and dove overboard. It was not until he hit the water that she realized that it was Sinbad.

"He is trying to save a water woman from the ocean," Henri muttered. "And people think I overact around women."

Sinbad dove as deep as he could, returned to the surface for a deep breath, and tried again. When he came to the surface again, he gasped deeply and felt a tap on his shoulder.

"What are you looking for?" Thoe asked. "I'll help look."

"You are alive!" Sinbad said thankfully.

"I let myself sink a few hundred feet when Tishimi threw me overboard. I saw you from below as you were diving. My kind often live on the sea bed. Poseidon himself has a huge palace on the ocean floor. I used to house sit for him when he was on vacation and walk his dogfish."

Sinbad understood little of what Thoe said, as he rarely did. She may have been insane, as the crew suspected, but he suspected there was more to her than that. She was not a true goddess, but she was still more from that world than his own. As he floated in the water with her, a distant memory struggled to come to the surface of his brain.

"I remember you!" Sinbad gasped.

"I should hope so," Thoe said. "It will make things go smoother at our wedding."

"I mean, I remember the first time I saw you. I was a child and trying to dive as far as I could underwater. I had my eyes closed, but when I opened them, I saw your two blue eyes shining. They illuminated your face. I had thought you were a dream or a hallucination. It was you, wasn't it?"

"You knew there had to be a reason why you named your ship as you did," Thoe smiled. "You had just never bothered to think of what it was before."

She summoned one of her waterspouts, and it carried them to the deck again. She glanced at Tishimi and smiled as she acknowledged the warrior woman with a nod. There was affection on her face and not anger. Tishimi was somewhat puzzled. At times, the nymph was a powerhouse of the ocean, and at other times she was meeker than a shy human woman. She had not helped at all when Proteus attacked, but had been a force of nature when she was saving Sinbad. She had also changed her appearance again, and her skin was a deep blue.

"The sea has many faces and moods," thought Tishimi. "She must as well."

"She made me love the sea," Sinbad said to Omar as he explained his recollection of his childhood memory. "I assumed she was a mermaid or a vision of one, and that image became our mascot."

Omar smiled at his friend. Omar had been married more times than he could remember. He always said it was six, but that was a best guess rather than a statistic. There was no logic to it, only emotion. Sinbad loved the sea, and this woman was as close to marrying the ocean as he could.

"Where are we going?" Omar asked.

"I have no idea," Sinbad admitted. "Thoe set the course. She could take us there herself if she wanted, so I did not argue."

"Then should we be concerned that the ship is starting to circle on its own?" Omar asked.

The Blue Nymph began to increase in speed and it was obvious they were caught in a giant whirlpool.

"Yes," Sinbad concurred.

The Blue Nymph was deposited roughly on the now-exposed sea bed. Out of the wall of water surrounding them stepped a twelve-foot-tall woman. A throne formed out of the sand and rose up to meet her. She wore brilliant white robes with golden jewelry. Her hair was as black as the night and her skin had the olive-skinned hue of Mediterranean people. She would have been intimidating at six inches tall. At twenty-four times that height, she was terrifying.

"Hi, mom," Thoe said sweetly. "I guess you heard?"

"I am Doris!" the giantess said in an echoing voice. "Daughter of titans, wife of a god, and mother of Thoe!"

"A terrifying woman with a horrible name," Omar whispered to Sinbad. "Typical mother-in-law, but I've had worse."

"Daughter!" Doris continued. "Are you insane?"

"If you were to take a vote," Thoe laughed, "yes. I have never claimed to be otherwise. My mind flows and ebbs like the water itself. Why does that matter mother?"

"He is a mortal!" Doris screeched. "And not just any mortal! A notorious rogue who has left broken hearts in every port and dead bodies behind him!"

Thoe pointed at the Blue Nymph.

"Do you see that magnificent ship? He built it and the magnificent carving on its prow in my honor and after seeing me only once as a child. It is now my temple, and I have a priest. I am planning a festival in my name! I am becoming complete because I met him!"

"Look," Doris said flatly," all men are like that in the beginning of a relationship. Your father was like that, and then after a few centuries he became a grumpy old man whose one joy in life is having people give him piggy back rides. This sailor will be the death of you."

"I am not like you," Thoe argued. "I am not immortal. I might live for a thousand years or more, but I will die."

"Not as fast as you will with him," Doris said ruefully.

"You are probably right," Sinbad stepped forward. "None of my crew is counting on reaching old age. I can give her adventure and a full life."

"And she can give you riches and an easy life," Doris accused.

"She can. But I am not going to ask her to do that. I prefer to live by my own wits. If she chooses to act, it will be on her own. She will not be expected to be our genie, granting our every wish."

Omar coughed loudly. Sinbad took the hint.

"The free salt is nice," Sinbad hurriedly added.

"You are a fool," Doris snarled. "You don't understand a single word I have said."

"Granted," Sinbad sighed. "I also do not understand most things Thoe says or does. I also can't predict everything that the sea does, and I love it with all of my heart."

"And you plan on going ahead with the wedding?" Doris asked.

"We are," Thoe said boldly. "It will be according to the customs of Sinbad's people and his entire crew will be in attendance."

"And probably a few of my enemies," Sinbad grimaced. His crew grinned. They were counting on that happening and were all planning on going fully armed.

"I will not attend," Doris stated. "And I will forbid all of your sisters from attending or it will be the death of them as well."

"Sisters?" Sinbad whispered to Thoe. "Don't you have any brothers?"

"One," Thoe said. "He's a shellfish. He won't come."

"I understand," Sinbad nodded. "I have a brother who's a jerk too."

"So, none of our family will attend?" Thoe said to her mother.

"Will there be an open bar?" Doris asked. Sinbad nodded. All bars at sailor weddings turn into open bars whether the hosts want them to be or not. He had decided to jump to the chase and simply start that way.

"Then your father will go," Doris said with a frown. She turned her attention to Sinbad. "You will have to be tested to prove your worthiness to marry my daughter."

"I already did that," Thoe said. "Giant monsters, loyalty, bravery. He passed."

"And the ritualistic testing of his tolerance to pain?" Doris said with a raised eyebrow.

"We haven't even kissed," Thoe said. "Let alone made love."

"That could be quite a honeymoon," Henri chuckled.

"Average," Omar said. "I've had worse."

"How does he express his affection for you?" Doris asked. Thoe took Sinbad's arm and put it firmly around her waist. Doris stared at the strange display for several seconds before speaking again.

"And he does that whenever you want him to?" Doris asked. Thoe nodded.

"That could catch on," Doris admitted. "And what about Proteus? I never liked him, but I can't imagine him admitting defeat easily."

Thoe recounted the combined force of the goddesses of many religions that had driven Proteus off.

"That sounds like Panacea," Doris reasoned. "She never wanted to be the goddess of universal remedy, you know, but they really didn't really need a goddess whose only role is to beat up jerky men."

There was the sound of water hitting a solid object as something big was forcing its way through the wall of water created by the sides of the whirlpool. It was unrecognizable at first, but the pincers that came forward made it clear.

"SO, NONE OF OUR FAMILY WILL ATTEND?"

It was a crab the size of two horses standing side by side. It made a beeline for Sinbad. His crew leaped into battle, with Tishimi leading the charge, her magical katana held high over her head with both hands, ready to split the crab's shell in two. She was only stopped by Sinbad's strong arms grabbing her from behind.

His crew backed off, assuming that Sinbad wanted to be the one to kill the creature. Instead, he stared at it. The crab did the same at him.

"Rafi!" called Sinbad. "Come here, slowly."

The healer obeyed, puzzled. He was the only crew member who was unarmed, and no help in a fight at the best of times.

"You know something of the stories of the Greek gods," Sinbad whispered. "Answer me this question."

Sinbad whispered the question to Rafi, who whispered back the answer. Sinbad approached the crab slowly.

"Nerites," Sinbad said politely. "I am pleased you are here. You can join the rest of your family, without the interference of me or my men."

The crab scuttled to where Thoe and Doris stood, smiling.

"This was another test, wasn't it?" Sinbad said. "I was supposed to think that your mother was the threat and she was summoning some monster to kill me. In reality, when you told me that your brother had been turned into a shellfish, I was supposed to figure out that was who this crab was."

'I wanted to see if you truly listened to me," Thoe admitted. "My mother would have stopped your crew from hurting him if you hadn't."

"And then this whirlpool would collapse on itself and we would have all been killed?"

"Possibly. Well, definitely the whirlpool would have collapsed," Doris admitted. "Whether or not you would have died was not my concern. Protecting my family was."

"And you wanted to know that I also meant your family no harm?" Sinbad continued. Doris nodded.

"Isn't that a bit extreme for a test to see if he was listening?" Haroun asked Omar. He had little experience with women or relationships.

"Slightly below average for that test," Omar commented. "And they only get harder the longer you have been married."

"Do you love my daughter?" Doris asked.

"I wish I could give you a definitive answer," Sinbad replied honestly. "I feel towards her like I have never felt to a woman, and I have never felt true love. I think that's what this is. I will never harm her in any way and will do my best to care for her always."

"No, she will harm herself," Doris muttered. "I am sure of it. I do not approve of this marriage, sailor, but I will not stop it. Remember the pledge you have just made to me that no harm will come to my daughter or you will suffer in ways you never dreamed of."

Sinbad bowed deeply to Doris. Thoe followed Sinbad back onto the Blue Nymph. As she went by Tishimi, the blue woman brushed against the warrior woman. Tishimi was shocked. It was like being hit with a brick.

"How was I able to flip her over the side of the ship so easily," Tishimi wondered. She followed her shipmates onto the ship, but took a last look back at Doris. There was a deep sadness in the giantess's eyes. She waved goodbye to Thoe as she held back her tears. Nerites also waved sadly at his sister. She did not think that a crab could show sorrow, but this one clearly was sorrowful.

Tishimi was worried. She had seen mothers in Japan act that way with their sons on many occasions; it was always when they sent their sons off to war, and they knew that they would never return home alive.

The Blue Nymph sailed along the coastline for several days. Not only did they have to find a mosque, they had to find a mosque that would allow Sinbad on the premises. Once that hurdle was passed, the priest was introduced to the bride, who usually cursed and chased her and Sinbad out of the mosque and the town. They finally found a temple in greater need of gold than Allah's constant approval. When the priest saw the wedding procession, he knew he should have held out for a higher price.

Thoe had received a new dress from her mother. It was not made of any known earthly material. It shone like the morning on a calm sea, and her blue eyes shone brighter than that.. Rafi walked closest to her, wearing Grecian-style robes. Nobody knew the true heritage of the healer, but he had obviously spent some time in Greece. It was a well-kept mystery if his time in Greece had been voluntary or not.

Sinbad looked like a prince in his robes. That should not have been a surprise, as he had once ripped them off a drunken prince who thought his royal title was a defense against Sinbad after enraging the sailor with numerous comments about his crew being related to farm animals. Few mosques would have allowed him to wear his scimitar, but compared to the rest of his crew he was positively dignified.

Rolf was proudly standing at his full height, which was over seven feet when his massive head of hair was taken into account. He was wearing what he considered his finest clothes: a worn bear skin that could not be washed but which he treasured for being from an animal he had killed with his bare hands.

He had polished his ax until it glittered in the sun as brightly as Thoe's dress.

Omar tried to force himself to smile, but it was not a successful effort. He was weary for many reasons. He had grown worried over Thoe's heritage. Then there was the issue over her claim of control of the ship. How unstable was she really, and how much was an act? He had also thought that such a public march through a town, even a backwater one such as this one, was a foolish risk to take when they knew that there were pirates in the vicinity. Lastly, the town and the mosque looked frighteningly familiar. He worried that he had been married there himself at least once, if not twice. He numbered a least two women in his list of enemies to watch out for.

Henri dressed like the prosperous Frenchman he once was before his life became an endless series of running out of one bedroom window after another with an ever-growing line of angry husbands behind him. He could have passed for a nobleman once, but his clothes were worn now and faded. His ego was not, however, and his attitude was more than enough to distract people from any holes his shirt might have.

Tishimi walked fiercely erect in her black silk pants and top, her three blades prominently displayed. She had been offered the chance to wear a dress equal in quality to Thoe's but had refused. She knew that she was a woman, and could not care less if her dress did not meet local standards of what a woman should wear. This was reinforced by William's presence directly behind her. The fierce Scotsman was wearing a kilt, with one hand constantly on the handle of his sword. Onlookers wondered how exactly he became Tishimi's father, but his stance made people believe that he was.

Next came the remainder of the crew, all heavily armed. Last in line was Haroun, who spent as much time keeping watch behind the procession as he did looking forward. The crew was doing its best to keep a lookout for any threats, but the town offered too many windows, doors, and alleyways that could be the launching point of a deadly attack at any second.

During the walk to the mosque, Sinbad stole side looks at Thoe. Her color was a lighter blue than when on the ship. He had never asked her about her color changes or the apparent changes in her mass. She had been spending more time in the ocean itself in the days leading up to their wedding, but he had learned that the nymph would tell him things on her own terms and not when he wanted her to. The fact that she did stand up to him was one of the things he had grown to love about her.

He froze on that thought. He had grown to love Thoe. He wanted to marry her.

They were about to enter the mosque when Henri stopped the procession. He was pointing ahead to a point behind the mosque in the distance. It was pirates, mainly the group that had tried to kill him. Sinbad was puzzled. The pirates were driving them back towards their own ship. It was then that Haroun called out an alert from the rear.

"Pirates!" the wiry lookout yelled. "They're blocking our return to the ship."

It was a variation of a pincer movement, leaving the crew of the Blue Nymph with no escape route. This was fine with the crew, as they had no intention of retreating. Sinbad, however, had instinctively put his arm around her waist, and instead of leaning into him she was leaning on him for support. She was very pale blue now and losing consciousness.

He glanced at his crew, and they had formed a circle around him and Thoe. They were prepared to fight to the death. They were disappointed when he gave his next command.

"Run!" he yelled. "Go west! Run parallel to the coast! Henri! You are the closest thing we have to a horseman! Steal us a mount and get me and Thoe behind you!"

Henri had been a decent rider back in France, but that had been several years previously. He did not think that any horse he could find would carry all three of them, but then he saw that he was carrying Thoe as if she were a doll. He helped Sinbad on the horse, with Thoe between them. He rode as fast as he could, but knew that the horse could not carry them far.

"As soon as you see another horse, stop and steal it!" Sinbad barked. "Our one hope is to keep going parallel with the coast until we have enough space between us and the pirates that we can head for the water safely!"

Henri found a second horse, but was quickly rushed by its owner. Before Henri could draw his own sword, Sinbad was upon the villager. With a viciousness that Henri had not seen before, Sinbad swung his scimitar with a blow that would have made Rolf and his ax jealous. The villager backed off immediately, his scimitar still vibrating from where Sinbad had struck it.

Henri dared to glance back. The crew had only partially obeyed Sinbad, but it was to their advantage. Some of the pirates had been forced to stay and battle the bloodthirsty sailors, while their grizzled captain led a small band to pursue Sinbad. It was essentially a posse, which made Henri smile. He had eluded such groups more times than he could count. When he passed a large barn, he swung his horse behind it to hide his change in direction. He had no idea why they were trying to reach the water when they were nowhere near the Blue Nymph, but he did not care. He counted on Sinbad to have a plan.

When they reached the shoreline, Henri cursed. He was unfamiliar with this area and had ridden to a cliff and not a beach. Sinbad did not criticize him in any way. He merely picked up the nymph, and running at full speed, jumped off the edge with Thoe in his arms.

The pirates were upon him now, but they were also frozen in shock by Sinbad's actions. Taking advantage of their pause, Henri attacked. There were four of them to his one, but he was acting more like Rolf than Rolf ever had. If the Viking had been present, he would have sworn that the Frenchman was a berserker. When he regained his senses, he was standing over three corpses and the bleeding captain. He roughly threw the head pirate over the back of the stolen horse and rode back towards the mosque.

Sinbad struck the water feet first. He had sailed these waters briefly years ago and knew that the water was deep. He allowed his momentum to carry him downwards quickly before he even tried to surface. He could easily swim while dragging Thoe along with him. The nymph was fading away to nothing. He took a long breath while keeping her below water and tied her roughly to his waist. He went below the surface again as deep as he dared, but still being able to resurface when needed. After several repeats, he miscalculated and dove too deep. He did not know if he resurfaced or not before he blacked out.

When Sinbad awoke, he was not sure what chocked him more: the fact that he woke up at all, the giant puncture marks on most of his body, or the fact that a giant crab was not only playing cards with several of his crew members but was winning consistently.

"Your brother-in-law is quite the character," Omar chuckled. He had rarely left Sinbad's side while his captain was recovering. "When we found you, he was holding you above water with one claw and Thoe under water with the other. Henri brought back the pirate captain, and he called off his dogs, and we sailed the Blue Nymph to where Henri last saw you. Nerites comes to check on you and Thole every day and to pick up some pocket money."

"Is Thoe alive?" Sinbad said as he sprung up in his bed.

"Alive, yes," Omar said. "Well, no. She insisted on not being taken from the ship until you were awake and knew you would survive. Her mom wanted to take her to Poseidon's castle to recover, but she refused. She's still weak so she spends all day in a cargo net under water except when we bring her up to give her a status report on you. She has something to tell you but won't tell us what it is."

Ignoring his pain, Sinbad jumped out of bed and made his way onto the deck. The crew was overjoyed to see him up and about but once they saw the determined look in his knew better than to try and stop him. Nerites waved at him with one claw while he raked in his winnings with his other.

He found the cargo net held by ropes over one of the railings. He tried to pull the net up himself, but Rolf stepped behind Sinbad to give some unseen assistance. Sinbad heard a weak "Hello" from Thoe when her head came above water. Sinbad flung himself over the side and fell beside the net, clinging to it. Thoe smiled at him. "Nice of you to drop in," she said with a smile. Her color was blue again, but not as dark as it once was.

"What happened?" Sinbad asked.

"My mother was right," Thoe admitted. "Marrying you was almost the death of me. As a nymph, my life force is drawn from nature, specifically the sea. I knew I was taking a chance walking on land when I took you to Panacea and going to the mosque, but I thought I could get away with it. Being onboard drained me, but slowly, and I could easily replenish it by taking dips in the ocean when nobody was looking. Tishimi probably saved my life when she threw me overboard, but don't tell her that. It would make her terribly sad."

"And when did you plan on telling me that being with me could kill you?" Sinbad asked.

"Once I told you my big news," Thoe smiled. "I'm pregnant. It turns out putting your arm around a nymph is all it takes. Who knew?"

"We will find a way to raise our child together, no matter what," Sinbad pledged. Thoe burst out laughing.

"Oh, Sinbad! I sometimes forget which one of us is insane! Of course I'm not pregnant! I thought it might cushion the blow that we may never see each other again."

Sinbad was now showing the shock Thoe had anticipated when she gave him her false news.

"My experiment of trying to live outside of the ocean was a failure," Thoe said. "When I first saw you, I knew that I had to try. I recognized you instantly as the boy I had seen years ago. In the moment our eyes locked, I could see the potential for true love. But sea creatures are not meant to be on dry land. That is why my mother forbade my family from coming to our wedding. It might have killed them."

"What about your father?"

"He showed up at the reception we planned and drank until he passed out. The disgusted hotel staff threw him into the ocean, hoping he'd drown. He's fine. Mother knew that he would be. They have a strong relationship even if they never see each other. Unfortunately, we have to see if we can do the same. I will have to spend months, if not years, at the bottom of the ocean after my adventure on dry land. I won't be able to leave and the pressure would kill you. Besides, you will forget me."

"How can I forget the owner of my ship?" Sinbad mused. "I will list you as such for the rest of my life. I will never forget you. And, we will see each other again."

Thoe shook her head. It was partially in disbelief of Sinbad's optimism and partially because she believed him to be wrong.

"You had forgotten that I existed or convinced yourself that I did not exist since the day you first saw me until I appeared on your ship!" Thoe exclaimed. "And I could live for centuries more. I will eventually forget you."

Sinbad slipped his arm through the webbing of the net and managed to put his arm around her waist. She sighed.

"OK," she relented, "I will remember that part. But I will be leaving soon. Nerites summoned our mother as soon as he saw you walking around. Your crew will never see him again either, but they probably won't mind after they realize that he cheats."

"Your mother hates me," Sinbad sighed. "How will she punish me when she arrives?"

"By taking me away," Thoe said. "In some ways, she respects you now. She knows that you risked your life to save me and that Nerites left you with a few scars. That might satisfy her."

"Might?" Sinbad asked suspiciously.

"There is a one in ten chance she might not kill you," Thoe agreed. "Don't ask about the odds of her not crippling you. You don't want to know."

"Whatever they are, I have faced worse odds," Sinbad said nonchalantly. Thoe raised an eyebrow in doubt but said nothing further

"Nerites saw you jump off the cliff with me," Thoe added. "He thought you'd die on impact, but you survived and then tried to save me. He was very impressed."

"I will have scars thanks to him for the rest of my life," Sinbad replied.

"He was impressed, not thrilled," Thoe amended. "My brother could have cut you in half, but he chose not to. He has been advocating on your behalf with my mother. He is a great ally for you. He would prefer it if Tishimi would quit drawing her sword every time she sees him. Why do you keep her? Is your ship and asylum as well as my temple?"

"It sometimes seems that way," Sinbad chuckled. "But I left Tishimi and the others to occupy as many of the pirates as they could so that we could make our escape. She can be an ally as well."

The water near them became disturbed as Doris made an appearance. She had chosen a slightly smaller form this time, but was probably still over eight feet tall. She ignored Sinbad and clapped her hands once. Nerites obediently scurried off of the ship with his ill-gotten gains.

"Are you up to the journey?" Doris asked.

"I am now," Thoe replied. "The crew of the Blue Nymph has taken care of me mother."

Doris winced at the name of the ship, but finally grunted and looked at Sinbad.

"You overstepped in naming your ship as you did, mortal," Doris snarled. "I have decided that you will keep your life and your ship, but know this: if you ever do anything that would dishonor my daughter's name, I will hunt you down no matter where you sail and rip you apart and feed you to the sharks. Are we clear?"

Sinbad bowed out of respect. He had crossed paths with many gods and supernatural beings in his voyages, but his potential mother-in-law was the scariest yet.

"I have also decided that you are to remain promised to my daughter in marriage. If she releases you one day, that is her choice. Remain faithful to her, Sinbad." The goddess's expression softened, but not by much. "I do want to have grandchildren someday, and there are worse things she could mate with in the ocean."

"That was a compliment," Thoe whispered. Sinbad bowed again in thanks.

"May I ask a question?" Sinbad asked softly.

"You just did!" Doris said. "What is your next one?"

"Is there any way Thoe and I could ever be together?"

"I have no interest in such things," Doris said dismissively. "Thoe's sisters and cousins might know, if you asked each of them. If you wish, I will tell all of them to take turns visiting you."

Thoe waved her hands in a sign of protest but Sinbad nodded in agreement. Doris was still laughing as she and Thoe sank into the depths.

When Sinbad returned to the deck, Rafi was waiting for him.

"You should have consulted me before you made your promise to Doris," the healer said. "Do you have any idea how many sisters Thoe has?"

Sinbad shook his head.

"Forty-nine!" Rafi laughed. "I don't know how many cousins Thoe has, but keep in mind that Doris is the youngest in a family of three thousand! By all accounts, Thoe is the sanest of the bunch!"

# The End

# Sailing With A Legend

Sinbad is a dream for writers and a nightmare for historians. Sinbad himself was a fictional character, of course, but part of the 1001 Arabian Nights stories. He was set in a real time period but with fantasy characters like the Rocs and the Old Man of the Sea. Since his debut, he has been used as a character in everything from Popeye cartoons to movies to a really bizarre Canadian tv show, because who better to interpret Arabian myths than the Canadians?

The universe of Sinbad is a series of cross-overs of characters and traditions that would give a comic book fan a wet dream. There are Vikings, and therefore all of their mythology and religion, Japanese samurai traditions and beliefs, French rogues with a touch of musketeer in them, Scottish warriors, Muslims, Christians, Greek Mythology and a touch of the tales of Homer. After all, why wouldn't a nymph from Greek mythology want to get married in a mosque while a bunch of pirates are chasing her?

I will not even bother to count the various anachronisms in my story, and I hope nobody else bothers to do so either. I do hope that they shift their suspension of disbelief into overdrive and wonder how Sinbad will defeat the Loch Ness Monster (or at least one of its relatives) and not worry how a crab could play a few hands of cards when it doesn't have hands.

According to Greek mythology, there are thousands of nymphs: spirits of nature associated with the sea, rivers, trees and various other natural locations. Three thousand! Three thousand creatures with powers far greater than humans that might be helpful or might be tricksters. Why shouldn't they all have a story?

I have no idea if it was possible for people of the different countries who make up Sinbad's crew to have met in the Eight century. That is when the original stories were set, but as the stories progressed, including the various films, the time periods became a bit more questionable. If we are going to have stories about monsters and mythical creatures, we may as well assume that the heroes all have time machines and that is how they were all able to meet. As long as the story is fast moving and fun, why should we stop and worry if it was possible?

**CARSON DEMMANS** - is a freelance writer in Regina SK, Canada. Since 1994, he has been published more than 1500 times, with sales varying from a single sentence for cartoon gags to newspaper columns, magazine articles, and short stories. He is the author of four books so far, with more in the works. The first three are regional humor, but his most recent one is OH MY GOD! THRY PRINTED THAT?, a history/satire of sexist and racist comic books. If you like books about pop culture history, check it out on Amazon or at Bear Manor Media. He needs the money.

# THE OLD MAN OF THE SEA

## by Terry Wijesuriya

The sharp sea breeze whipped the colorful awnings of the many stalls that lay a house's width away from the harbor of Tyndis. The harbour itself was astir with the ships and boats that came in every day, from all ends of the earth. The majority of crafts were small dhows and sampans, lying low in the water as their crews unloaded the country goods they'd brought from the neighboring ports. Men of all shades of brown, and some other shades too, thronged the waterfront.

Among the bustle two ships stood out. One was a yathra dhony, a large outrigger craft, with planks that were sewn together. Its lateen sails were furled, and men were busy on board, replacing the old cadjan roofing of its cabin. The dhony caught the eye of many a casual onlooker, towering as it did above the country craft around it. Some people speculated where it had come from, but most people knew, and therefore did not venture to talk about it.

Even the dhony, however, was dwarfed by yet another craft that lay at anchor, creaking gently with the waves. In marked contrast to the other craft in the harbour, this ship lay silent and empty. Yet no man dared approach it too closely. An elegant ship of Persian build, the craft was only slightly larger than the dhony, yet conveyed a sense of richness and power that was beyond the humbler ship. The Persian craft bore no more than a passing resemblance to other ships; it gave the impression of having been improved upon until it was the best ship it could be. Its prow was an exquisitely carved maiden, starkly distinguishing itself from the Muslim-owned craft in harbour, which remained plain and unadorned out of religious deference. Yet it was not this that caused people passing by to avert their eyes and make various signs to ward off the evil eye. No, the cause for their fear was something else-something seemingly innocuous. For in the sea breeze, which came through the rigging and ropes of all the craft at harbour, lifted the limp triangular sail of the Persian ship and displayed it to all passers-by. The sky blue of her sail sent a shock of fear into those who knew, and a sense of foreboding into those who didn't. And the old sailors who had been from one end of the Indian Ocean to the other spat away from the harbour, cursing the men who had brought the Blue Nymph to Tyndis.

A slender man of medium height, the lower part of his face concealed behind the end of a flowing scarf, shouldered his way through the crowds that thronged the market street and came face-to-face with a woman who sat behind a table near the doorway to a building.

"Bhavika," the man said, greeting her. He had done business with her ever since the death of her husband, whose business she carried on.

"My lord," she replied, courteously.

"I would like the usual," he said.

"I'm afraid it's taken," she replied, not meeting his eyes.

He stared at her for an instant, not believing his ears. He leaned his weight on the table.

"Excuse me?" he asked, softly.

"You can't have the room," Bhavika said, looking up and making eye contact.

"Why can't I?" he demanded.

"It's in use."

"By who?" he asked, between gritted teeth.

"Someone who is paying well for the privilege," Bhavika said.

"Who pays better than I? Who pays better than Jalasti on the whole coast here?" he asked, throwing an arm out.

"There are others," she said calmly.

Jalasti unwound his scarf from his face, revealing a lean face with sharp features, topped by spiky black hair. He stared steadily at Bhavani, who met the challenge of his clear brown eyes without flinching.

"Tell me, Bhavani," he said, almost purring. "Who is more important than Jalasti in these parts?"

Bhavani regarded him in silence for a while, and then leaned forward.

"Jalasti thinks he is a big man," she murmured, "but Jalasti forgets that the world is bigger than the round trip from Tyndis to Mannar. There are other names that shake the entire ocean- that cause tsunamis to touch lands further than you have ever been."

"And what is that name?" asked Jalasti.

"Sinbad," Bhavani said.

"I don't understand why we need to confront them?" Aida asked, half-running to keep up with Jalasti as he strode angrily from the harbour. They made an odd pair, the slim man in the tunic and scarf and the tall girl with the shoulders of an archer and her hair in long braids.

"He has taken my place," Jalasti frowned horribly.

Aida sighed and slowed her walk. "Is that it?" she demanded, coming to a complete halt.

Jalasti swung round and looked up at her. "What do you mean, is that it? Isn't that enough?"

"I thought he had attacked you, or one of the men, from the way you were acting. If this is just an ego thing I'm leaving my bow in the ship."

"No!" Jalasti threw himself in her way. "Bring it; we will need every ounce of firepower we have to face that crew of bloodthirsty men."

"Jalasti, you know, and I know, that this is all about scaring Sinbad and his crew. If you actually wanted to fight, you would have brought the rest of the crew too. But I'm telling you, we'd better either go prepared to fight or go completely unarmed. We don't want to tread on the toes of someone like Sinbad."

"Why should Jalasti be afraid of treading on some Sindhi riff-raff?" Jalasti almost howled with anger.

"You are being extremely foolish, and I absolutely refuse to come with you and bring my bow," Aida said, sternly, and she started for the ship, brushing Jalasti out of her way with minimum effort.

Powerless to stop her, Jalasti watched her go. When she was almost at the dhony, however, the earth moved. Disoriented, Jalasti went sprawling on the road and stayed there, expecting something worse to happen. He saw Aida lose her balance, but she regained it and began running back towards him. He struggled to his feet.

"What's wrong?" he called, as she sprinted closer.

"The town!" she yelled, and then she was past him, and his eyes followed her.

From the centre of the town, from which they had so recently come, a tall pillar of fire stretched up to the blue skies.

Sinbad el Ari yawned hugely. He gestured to the serving girl to pour some more drink for him, and then he looked around at his crew. They all sprawled across the largest room in the eating house, which he had procured with surprisingly little trouble. He always expected to have to butt horns with local dignitaries for the choicest rooms, but that hadn't happened here.

Ralf and Haroun were squabbling over the last dishes of food, leftover from their meal. Rafi had fallen asleep in the corner of the room. Omar had asked the serving girl something and was now talking to her in a low tone. To judge from the girl's feigned horror and bashfulness, Omar was laying plans early for the rest of his stay. Byrne and Henri were deep in discussion about something else, and Tishimi…Sinbad started. Where was Tishimi?

The daytime sound of the people in the streets suddenly shifted. The light changed, and Sinbad became aware of a low-pitched drone, low enough to be almost inaudible, but just loud enough to set his teeth on edge. Judging by the way his crew leapt to their feet, their teeth had been set on edge too.

The door burst open. Tishimi stood there, her black silk robe still swirling with the speed she had run there with.

"There is…something strange," she said, calmly. "You had all better come and see."

Three stalls in the market had been burst asunder. The food and goods they had held lay scattered across the ground, but no street children scrambled for them. Everyone in the area stood transfixed, staring at the enormous pillar of fire that rose out of a jagged, blackened hole in the ground.

It moved and burnt in the living way of fire, and the air around it on all sides shimmered. The already hot day became hotter as the crew approached the pillar of flame.

"Don't touch it, it is sacred fire," a voice warned, as Ralf walked towards it, mesmerized. The enormous Norseman scowled and swung around.

"Do you think I am afraid of touching sacred fire?" he demanded.

"I think nothing of the sort," the voice retorted, and the crowd shifted for an old shark-charmer to come forward. "I think, though, that you are not worthy to touch the sacred fire. None of us are," he added, seeing Ralf's face darken.

"Why is there sacred fire here?" Sinbad asked, stroking his beard. "Why did it appear?"

"If we knew, it would not be sacred," the shark-charmer said, to sniggers from the crowd.

Sinbad's crew bristled at the sound of the crowd's amusement.

"Shall I teach the old jackal a lesson?" Omar grunted, fingering the handle of his sword.

Sinbad raised a hand, and the crew subsided.

"Old one," he turned respectfully to the shark-charmer. "What do you think about this sacred fire? Is it a sign of good fortune?"

The shark-charmer stared piercingly at Sinbad. "It is on the contrary the sign of the worst luck you have ever faced, Sinbad el Ari."

"How does he know…" Haroun gasped, but Rafi elbowed him in the ribs. "Everybody knows, stupid. Hold your tongue and wait."

"You have weathered many storms, Sinbad, but this one will be the worst. For you have faced many enemies before, both of this world and of other worlds. But this time, you will face the lord of all fears, the source of all sailors' nightmares. The Old Man of the Sea is awake, Sinbad, and he is looking for you."

"And so am I!" A new voice cut across the shark-charmer's as his words fell into the silence of the crowd.

The crowd parted hastily, leaving a clear space between Sinbad's crew on the one hand and a slim man with a naked blade on the other. A tall woman with a bow stood behind him, looking taken aback. The tall pillar of flame shot up on the left. The man took a step forward, towards Sinbad.

Henri's arrow left his bow as soon as the man's heel touched the ground. He fully expected to see the man drop bonelessly, his heart pierced by the arrow, but Henri had reckoned without the woman behind. Although clearly at a disadvantage, evidently taken aback by the man's sudden challenge, she pushed him aside and in the same fluid motion, drew an arrow from her quiver, nocked it to the bow, and was releasing it as Henri's arrow buried itself harmlessly in the ground near her.

The man with her continued to run, shouting and waving his sword wildly. The crowd muttered as they watched him run. Sinbad glanced at his crew. Henri was nocking another arrow, but the others were watching him out of the corners of their eyes, waiting to take a cue from him.

"Henri and I will handle this," he said, curtly. "Cut in if more turn up."

The others stepped backwards, and Sinbad turned to face the maniac alone.

He drew his scimitar, its long, curved blade flashing in the sun and the firelight. The man kept on at a run, although it was obvious to everyone watching that his old, weathered sword was nowhere near the caliber of Sinbad's. Their blades met in a clash of steel. Sinbad was feeling lenient, and more than a little perplexed, so he parried rather than going on the offense. They fenced in this manner for some time.

"Fight, damn you!" the madman raged.

"I don't fight the insane," said Sinbad, suavely, sidestepped a wild swing.

"I am not insane!" the man shouted, accompanying each word with hacks and slashes that cut through thin air.

"Then why are you attacking me in this foolish manner if you aren't?"

"Why am I attacking you? Why am I attacking you?" the man shouted. "You have the gall, the effrontery to ask me that?" He seemed exhausted now, and his sword arm fell, the edge of his unblooded sword trailing in the dust.

"I usually like to know why before I kill my attackers."

"You scorn me," the man accused. "You deliberately spit in my face, and steal my possessions."

Sinbad thought for a moment, then shrugged. "You're going to have to be more specific. There are hundreds of people around the place who could say something similar."

Henri and the other archer, after trading as many arrows as they could, had become aware of the discussion going on between Sinbad and the man and had drifted over, untouched.

"I," the man announced, grandly, "am Jalasti."

Sinbad scratched his head.

"And I am Sinbad," he said, after the silence had gone on for a little longer than was necessary.

Jalasti cried out in frustration. "Everyone knows that you are Sinbad," he yelled angrily, "but Sinbad ought to know that there are others important to Tyndis. Sinbad need not assume that he will get everything he wants, as if Tyndis lies in wait for Sinbad to give it life and meaning."

Slowly the light began to dawn in Sinbad's mind. This was the storm he had wrongly expected before their meal. This was the local grandee, now slighted by the mere fact of Sinbad's experience and renown.

"I cannot fight you," Sinbad declared.

"Why? Do you think that I am not a match for you?" Jalasti asked.

Sinbad's forehead creased for a moment. "Yes, I do think that."

"Do you think that there is no one here in this part of the ocean who can match you?" Jalasti spat in his rage.

"Not necessarily," Sinbad mused. "It's just that…in terms of handling a sword, a physical fight, I mean…I do think that we are not evenly matched."

Jalasti's answer was a howl of rage, and Sinbad's eyes lit up with a devilish gleam as he saw the men in the crowd preparing to fight. Jalasti's crew, he assumed, which meant his crew would finally get a look in on the action.

They were already on it, unsheathing their weapons and coming forward to stand in a loose semi-circle around Sinbad.

Aida heaved a sigh. Jalasti waved his sword and started forward again, and all hell broke loose.

Aida, loosing off arrow after arrow, became aware that Henri was matching her speed. She stared at him, and he looked directly into her eyes, nocking an arrow to his string and aiming it at her with a smile. She narrowed her eyes and dodged, never faltering in her own aim and rate of fire.

The crowd surged back and forth. The timider among them left hurriedly, and the others joined the free-for-all. The individual melees were lapping around the place where Aida stood, and soon she was in the thick of things where her bow would be of no use. She hung it over her shoulder and whipped out one of her wickedly sharp arrows, using it as a dagger whenever anyone tried to get her involved. She saw Omar fighting past her, calling down curses upon anyone and everyone in a grumbling undertone as he slashed his way through the opposition. Haroun and Byrne whirled past, backs to each other as they parried and cut at everyone who came within reach. Aida ignored them, focusing on reaching Jalasti and fighting next to him. They had a tremendous advantage, which was that there were only two people…Aida and Jalasti…on their side. Everyone else was an enemy, which Sinbad's crew had not yet figured out. The rest of the crowd had joined in for various reasons; revenge on Jalasti and his crew, revenge on Sinbad, although he had just come into port, and sheer love for a fight.

Aida skirted around two people dueling furiously with short krises and then slammed so hard into something that she lost her breath. She craned her neck to see the face a full head above her not inconsiderable height. Seeing Ralf in action was an awe-inspiring sight. His double-headed battleaxe was wet with blood, and as she watched, his fingers slipped on the drenched handle and he flung it away with a grunt. She dodged away slightly, and saw him pick up a man bodily and use him as a battering ram to knock several more down.

She was carried away again, and caught sight of Jalasti just ahead of her. Sinbad was toying with him as a cat toys with a mouse, pricking him slightly now and again to remind him of who was boss, but otherwise letting the other man think they had a fair fight. Aida tightened her grip on the arrow in her hand and adjusted her bow across her shoulder. Before she could take a step forward, however, a figure in flowing black robes materialized in front of her.

Aida stared as Tishimi pulled a short dagger out of her sash. She moved in a way Aida had not seen before, and at first her defences were completely down. Fortunately for her, Tishimi too seemed off-balance, and before she recovered, Aida had slashed down with her arrow. The other girl danced away, and Aida whirled around to face her.

"So you're a woman too," Tishimi stated, conversationally.

Aida grunted, surprised that the other was starting a conversation at a time like this.

"Did they let you on the ship without making a fuss?" Tishimi asked. "Because I had the devil of a time getting everyone round to it."

"I get blamed for storms a lot," Aida admitted. Her arrow slashed down again, deflected by Tishimi's dagger.

Tishimi nodded, sympathetically. "Happens," she agreed, feinting with her dagger and bringing her bare hand up in the sword-hand to chop at Aida's neck. Aida straightened up, catching the blow on her shoulder. It was still powerful enough to make her lose her balance, and she almost went headlong onto the ground.

Avoiding Tishimi's dagger descending towards her, she regained her balance.

"Look, I need to help my captain," she explained, through gritted teeth.

"Oh, well, you see, your captain is kind of engaged with mine," Tishimi smiled as she drove Aida back again. "So I cannot let you go, because that will put my captain at a disadvantage."

Aida set her jaw and lunged forward.

For the next few minutes, both concentrated on their battle.

"Where's your archer boy?" Aida asked, deliberately insulting in her tone.

Tishimi just smiled. "He bested you, did he?"

"As a matter of fact, he didn't," Aida snarled. "But I think I see him going along the harbour road there." She jerked her head in the direction of the harbour.

"Please, do you really think I would fall for that?"

Aida shrugged. "Do you really think I would use such a pathetic ruse?"

Something in her tone made Tishimi put on a spurt of energy. She maneuvered Aida around so that she could keep her in sight while looking along the harbour road. She saw Henri hurrying along the road, away from the town and the melee.

"What on earth?" she muttered, and her instant of surprise was enough for Aida, who jabbed at her wrist with the feathered end of the arrow. Tishimi's hand fell numb, and her dagger fell to the ground. Aida sprang away, joining Jalasti where he stood in one place, holding his sword up with both hands now as Sinbad needled him with blade and voice.

Aida and Jalasti were back to back, and Sinbad's crew was returning to form up around their captain. Most of the other combatants had either retired, dead or injured, or taken up individual quarrels with other members of the crowd. Of Sinbad's crew, only Rafi and Henri were missing. The others came together to surround Jalasti and Aida, Tishimi wringing her hand but soon pulling a long sword out with her other hand.

"Ambidextrous, eh?" Aida called to her. Tishimi responded by winking and slashing her sword through the air a few times.

"I'm tired of this," Sinbad announced. "I will end your miserable career, Jalasti. Your name will be known across the seas, but only because I killed you."

"You damned foreigners think you can come here and be the big man," Jalasti's voice was shaking with exertion. He was soaking with sweat and blood.

"Foreigners?" Aida hissed at him. "What are we?"

Sinbad heard, and laughed. "Your first mate fights better than you do," he complimented, generously.

Aida spat at him. "I know she does," Jalasti retorted, "that's why she's here."

"Too bad both of you will fight no more," Sinbad looked up. "Tishimi, would you like to finish her off?"

Tishimi ran her finger across the edge of her sword and smiled.

"I will take this Jalasti," Sinbad swung his scimitar a few times to limber up his wrist.

*At least I will fall to a decent foe,* Aida thought, and steeled herself to take as many of them with her as possible.

Tishimi cut at her, and Aida's arrow fell apart, cut through as cleanly as the waves before a prow. She frantically grabbed at her quiver, but she knew she would never make it in time. Her hand was still empty when she looked up and saw Tishimi's strangely gleaming blade sliding through the air towards her.

Time seemed to slow down. Sinbad noticed that his planned killing blow was moving through the air as if it were underwater, and Jalasti's eyes bulged as he saw the blade coming down at him. The rest of the crew saw it at the same time…a glowing field of blue around Jalasti and Aida. Sinbad and Tishimi's weapons slowed down as they approached the blue glow, and when they struck it, there was a brief flash as of lightning. The swords fell with a clatter.

With the sound, the pillar of fire which had been burning unchecked and unregarded throughout the melee suddenly roared higher, and switched abruptly into a great geyser of water. It hung in the air like a column for an instant, and then rushed down upon the figures standing below.

Sinbad felt himself rising through the water. He kicked up, trying to break the surface, but he couldn't. It felt almost as though the water was holding him. He panicked, unable to breathe, and then suddenly he could. It seemed to him that he was still inside the water.

*SINBAD,* came a voice, deep and booming like the breakers on rocks.

"Uh," said Sinbad.

*YOU WILL NOT KILL THEM,* the voice said.

"Why not?" asked Sinbad, irritated.

*THEY HAVE SERVED THEIR PURPOSE AND WILL DO SO AGAIN. NO, SINBAD, RATHER, LOOK TO YOUR SHIP AND YOUR CREW.*

"Wait!" shouted Sinbad, feeling the water changing around him. "Who are you?"

The voice did not reply, merely laughed, and its laughing was terrible, like the sucking of a whirlpool.

Then Sinbad couldn't breathe again, and he felt himself sinking. He made one last superhuman effort to break away, and then everything went black.

"I tell you, I don't care what the voice told you," Tishimi said, for the umpteenth time. "They should be killed, they are clearly in league with whatever that voice was."

Sinbad shook his head somberly. They stood on the harbour. It was night,

"SINBAD FELT HIMSELF RISING IN THE WATER."

and the stars in their brilliance lit the pier as if it were day.

"Load them in," he ordered. Ralf carried Aida and Jalasti on board the Blue Nymph. They were both still unconscious, and trussed tightly with ropes.

"Where are we going?" Omar asked, quietly.

"Jalasti will tell us, I have no doubt," Sinbad said. "We may have to, uh, *persuade* him a little."

"Look, Sinbad, I'm as much in favour of finding Rafi and Henri and the rest of the crew as you are. But we need to kill these two. Who knows what other powers they can call down?" Tishimi cautioned.

"And how will we ever know where to start looking if we kill them now? We get all the information we need from them, and *then* you can kill them if you wish," Sinbad compromised.

Tishimi looked unconvinced. Omar spoke up.

"I don't like the idea of having another woman on board," he ignored Tishimi's glare.

Sinbad shrugged his powerful shoulders. "I want to keep an eye on both of them. Also, I find it odd that their crew hasn't come to look for them yet."

"What was their ship anyway?" Omar turned to look at the other ships in the harbour. The harbour looked strangely emptier than earlier in the day.

Some sounds drifted up from the hold.

"All right, Ralf?" Omar called down.

"No," Ralf shouted, his voice muffled. "This fellow is awake and giving me trouble."

"Send him back to sleep," Omar started suggesting, but Sinbad forestalled him.

"Bring him back up then. Let the girl stay below for now," he ordered the Norseman.

Ralf returned, dragging Jalasti by one arm. Jalasti's legs had been untied, but his arms were bound behind him and Ralf kept a very tight grip on his arm.

"What the devil is all this?" Jalasti asked, angrily.

Sinbad strode up to him and stared into his eyes. Jalasti met his gaze unflinchingly.

"I could ask you the same," Sinbad said, shortly. "Where are my crew members?"

Jalasti shrugged insolently. "How should I know? They all decided to get involved in what should have been a fight between you and I. Is it my fault if they go missing afterwards?"

"What did you do with them?" Sinbad was getting quieter but more menacing.

"I did nothing with them that you didn't see," Jalasti said, scornfully.

Sinbad sighed. "Jalasti, two of my crew members have disappeared and you are responsible. Tell me where you've kept them."

"I tell you, Sinbad, I have nothing to do with this."

"My patience is wearing thin. You have a very short while to tell me what I want to know before I lose it entirely."

Jalasti rolled his eyes elaborately, turning his head as he did so. In an instant, his demeanor changed.

"Where the devil is my ship?" he blurted out.

"What do you mean?" Sinbad asked.

"Oh, I see it now," Jalasti said, bitterly. "The mighty Sinbad couldn't bear the thought of someone else, someone lesser than he working these waters. You've scuttled my ship, you damned filthy seadog!"

Omar and Tishimi, watching from behind their captain, saw the muscles on his neck swell.

Sinbad pushed his face close to Jalasti's. "WHERE HAVE YOU KEPT MY MEN?" he bellowed, causing even Ralf to flinch slightly.

Jalasti didn't turn a hair, but bellowed back. "WHY DID YOU SCUTTLE MY SHIP?"

"I'VE HAD IT WITH YOUR OBSTINACY, YOU MISBEGOTTEN SON OF A DONKEY. TELL ME WHERE YOUR PRECIOUS OLD MAN OF THE SEA HAS TAKEN MY MEN!" Sinbad roared, spit flying.

Jalasti looked shocked. "The Old Man of the Sea took them?"

"Yes," Sinbad was breathing heavily while lowering his voice.

Jalasti looked for a moment as if he might faint.

"Tell me where he is?"

"If the Old Man of the Sea has taken your crewmates, and if the Old Man of the Sea has taken my ship, there is nothing for us to do. Write off our losses and leave, maybe," Jalasti looked defeated.

"Aren't you in league with him?" Sinbad was confused.

Jalasti stared back, and finally started laughing weakly. "In *league*? With the Old Man of the Sea?"

Sinbad's eyebrow twitched. "Explain yourself without laughing!"

Jalasti stopped and wiped his mouth. "Sorry about that, but no one is in league with the Old Man of the Sea."

"Who is he then? And why has he taken my men?"

"He...I don't know if he is a 'he' or not. A being. He lives in the sea, between here and Mannar. No one is in league with him. He does as he pleases and takes what he wants."

"And you just let him?"

Jalasti shrugged as best he could with Ralf hanging on to his arm. "There is nothing we can do. The local people call them sacrifices…if you go into the sea at certain points, if you sail on certain routes or if you carry certain objects the sea will take a sacrifice of you."

Sinbad scowled. "And you say the Old Man of the Sea has taken Rafi and Henri?"

"And my ship," Jalasti reminded him.

Sinbad abruptly turned and walked away.

Omar stepped forward. "Sinbad, shall we…"

Sinbad spun around. "We're going to find this Old Man of the Sea," he said, his voice carrying to the rest of the crew.

Jalasti sighed.

"Where can we find him?" Sinbad demanded.

"Well, we usually avoid the middle of the sea. I mean we travel along the coast, keeping it in sight the whole way, and then get round to Mannar. The Old Man of the Sea lives further out at sea so he won't bother people who stay close to the land."

"So we will strike straight out for Mannar and hopefully will encounter the Old Man en route," Sinbad decided.

Jalasti shook his head just as Omar nodded.

"Bad idea, Sinbad. I mean, personally I think it's a bad idea to confront the Old Man at all, but since you seem determined… Anyway, I have a garrison of Abyssinian archers. Aida's countrymen. They're at my place on Mannar, and if we can pick them up they have special arrows they use for situations like this."

Sinbad scowled, deep in thought. "Right, Omar," he turned, "let's set sail tonight."

Jalasti was shaking his head again.

"What now?" Sinbad asked, exasperated.

"We can't go in the Blue Nymph," Jalasti replied.

"Why the devil not?"

"Because I have a bit of a… situation."

"What kind of a situation?"

"Well," Jalasti began, reluctantly, "this ship has nails."

Omar cocked his head to one side.

"So what?" Ralf asked, his voice booming down.

Jalasti had forgotten about him. "So, uh, ships with nails can't come anywhere near Mannar," he explained.

Sinbad sighed again. "Jalasti, please tell me why not in one sentence, without dragging this out. Rafi and Henri are missing, and I would like to get them back before the Old Man of the Sea kills them or whatever."

A sound from the hold drifted up.

"Oh, Aida," Tishimi remembered. She looked at the big Scotsman, "Would you go and bring her up to join this conversation, Byrne?"

The stocky Scot made his way to the hold, and the others resumed the conversation.

"I would really rather not tell you," Jalasti picked up. "Couldn't you take my word for it?"

"No," Sinbad declared. "I could not."

"All right. It's a magnetic fort. You can't approach with metal ships because the metal will all fly out and the ship will sink."

Sinbad raised one eyebrow skeptically.

Omar cut in. "That's so, Sinbad, there are similar magnetic forts around these parts. I've heard tell of them."

"I suppose the ships sink very close to land, so that people can go out and, ahem, *salvage* goods from them?" Sinbad inquired.

Jalasti shrugged gracefully. "You know how it is."

"So we can't approach Mannar in the Blue Nymph," Omar said. "Yet we'll need your archers to confront the Old Man of the Sea."

"We can take the Blue Nymph to Uratthurai, and take country boats from there to Mannar," Jalasti suggested. "Then we bring the archers back with us to board the Blue Nymph and then we head straight out to sea and face the Old Man of the Sea."

Sinbad looked at him suspiciously. He glanced at Omar, who nodded very slightly. He looked at Tishimi, who also nodded. He made up his mind.

"Omar, get the crew ready. We sail for Uratthurai tonight."

The journey to Uratthurai took far longer than Sinbad would have liked. Jalasti insisted that they travel hugging the coastline, and Omar insisted that they do as Jalasti suggested. Sinbad was all for confronting the Old Man of the Sea as soon as possible, but the others voted him down and eventually he was forced to give in.

The days passed monotonously. The whole crew of the Blue Nymph was on edge because they didn't enjoy the prospect of facing the Old Man of the Sea without Rafi and Henri. Jalasti and Aida likewise because they didn't enjoy the reality of being virtual prisoners. Tishimi didn't lose a single opportunity to remind Sinbad that the two strangers might be pawns of the Old Man of the Sea, and she never bothered to hide her distrust from Jalasti and Aida.

Several times, Haroun called a warning as small country boats appeared from around sharp curves and mouths of rivers, and drew near the Blue Nymph with lightning speed. Upon reaching the ship, however, they almost always halted abruptly and drifted back to where they had come from. That this had something to do with the fact that Jalasti was always prominently visible on board the ship never crossed anyone's mind; although Omar did watch keenly for any sign that Jalasti knew the people in the boats.

One morning, however, the boats didn't halt. They shot at a frightening rate towards the Blue Nymph. Sinbad didn't utter a word, but his crew all appeared on deck, armed as usual to the teeth.

"Pirates!" Byrne breathed.

Jalasti shot him a look, but said nothing.

The woman in the leading boat stood up in the stern, holding out her empty hands to show she was unarmed.

"What do you want?" Omar shouted, after a look at Sinbad.

"We need to speak with Jalasti," the woman called.

"You know them, Jalasti?" Sinbad jerked his head towards the people in the boats.

"Of course," Jalasti answered. "*I* am not a stranger to these parts."

He went forward. He had just begun talking with the woman when Sinbad interrupted.

"Perhaps it would be best for all of us if you invited her on board," he said, suavely.

Jalasti whipped his head around to look at Sinbad.

Aida licked her lips and tried to surreptitiously to crack her joints. She knew that Sinbad was making the suggestion in order to eavesdrop on what Jalasti and the woman were talking about, and she knew equally well that Jalasti knew this. She also knew that if Jalasti decided he didn't want Sinbad to hear, he and she would have to once again fight their way out of a tough corner.

To her relief, Jalasti spoke a few words to the woman and then turned back to Sinbad.

"We will talk on shore. You may join us."

The meeting took place on the nearby beach. The people from the boats, the crew of the Blue Nymph and Aida thronged around as Jalasti, Sinbad and the woman sat cross-legged together.

"There is something strange afoot, Jalasti," the woman spoke as though Sinbad weren't there. Sinbad frowned slightly, but remained at ease, content to listen.

"Such as?" Jalasti queried.

"One of the boats that went out some days ago failed to return."

"Drowned?"

"No," the woman shook her head decisively. "The people in her were much too experienced to have drowned on a day when the sea was as calm as the Milk Ocean."

"Perhaps the ship they were trying to take had Abyssinians on board," Aida put in.

The woman glanced up. "Oh, Aida! I didn't notice you. But no, you are mistaken. There was indeed a ship, but the boat was not close enough to it when it disappeared."

"How do you know?" Jalasti asked.

"There was a witness. Hana, come here." She turned and gestured to the people from the boats. A child of about six years old came forward.

"Tell these people what you saw that day," the woman instructed, giving the child a gently push.

The child said nothing, but stared around at the crowd with big eyes. She seemed especially taken with Ralf, craning her neck backwards to look at the blond giant.

"Come, Hana, tell us," Jalasti coaxed.

The girl looked around at Jalasti, seeming surprised. "I had kanji for breakfast that day," she said, suddenly. "Then my father went in the boat with the others. But he promised me if I behaved myself I would go with him, but when he went he didn't take me. So I went with my two friends…one of them lives in that house there;" here she pointed to one of the huts at the edge of the beach. "Ad the other one lives over there." The second friend's house was evidently out of sight, for the child twisted herself around to point at the far end of the village.

"Never mind where your friends live," the woman prodded. "Tell the story."

"I went with my two friends to the beach, and…" The child's voice trailed off, and she looked anxiously at the crowd.

"What happened?" Jalasti asked.

"My mother will punish me," the child whispered.

"She will not," the woman promised. "I will make sure she won't."

Reassured, the child picked up the thread of her tale. "We went and we took my big brother's boat. It's a small boat so the three of us can take it out alone. We got inside and we started to go out of the river into the sea where my father and the others in the big boat went. We got to the edge of the sea and all the mangroves are there and then the boat got stuck in the roots because we didn't know how to push it to the middle. So then we were climbing on the mangroves trying to get it free, but I was scared that my father and the others would go out of sight before we could follow them. So I told my friends to push the boat free, and I climbed to the top of the mangroves to look for the big boat."

She took a deep breath.

"Then what?" the woman prompted her.

"I saw the boat, and I saw the big ship with all the presents, and then…and then,,, there was a big huge fire and a booming voice said something. Then I got scared, but I was watching, and then there was a loud noise and then the ship and the boat disappeared."

There was silence for a while.

"Just disappeared?" Sinbad asked.

The girl turned and stared frankly at him. "Yes."

"Did they sink?" Omar questioned.

"No," the girl said, scornfully. "I know ships suck the sea when they sink. This one didn't sink, but it disappeared with my father's boat. The sea took them as a sacrifice. I don't know where they are now."

"This voice," Sinbad urged, "what did it sound like?"

"A grandfather," the child said. "A big old grandfather, like Grandpa Fahid."

"And what did the voice say?" Jalasti asked, eagerly.

"I don't know. I told you, it sounded like Grandpa Fahid."

Jalasti and Sinbad turned to the woman.

"What language does this Grandpa Fahid speak?" Sinbad inquired eagerly. "Between my crew we can manage quite a few."

The woman shook her head and gestured towards the crowd, which parted slightly for a wizened old man to come forward. He gave them a big grin, flashing his toothless gums.

Jalasti and Sinbad groaned and turned back.

"You couldn't understand anything the voice said, at all?" Aida asked the child. She solemnly shook her head, and then went over to Ralf.

"Can you put me on your head?" she asked, politely. "I want to see your white hair."

The village persuaded Sinbad and the others to stay for a meal, although it was very evident that the invitation had only been offered because of Jalasti's presence.

Ralf had been commandeered by the children and was obediently sitting in their midst, as they climbed over his big frame. The others were making the most of a free meal when Aida slipped away from the cheery village fires and went down the beach.

She sat near a dune that hid her from the sight of anyone in the village. Out in the deeper waters, the Blue Nymph lay at anchor. Sinbad had insisted that the whole crew return to the ship at night instead of remaining on shore, but for now only Haroun was on board, standing guard. The crescent moon and stars shone softly down over the sea, which was occasionally wrinkled by a lace-edged wave. Aida slid her bow and quiver off her shoulder and clasped her hands over her knees. Her mind was working furiously.

It seemed clear enough that the ship and boat had been taken 'as a sacrifice' by the Old Man of the Sea. But that didn't make their course of action any clearer. Sinbad seemed content to throw his entire crew at the Old Man of the Sea, without having any idea of how to defeat him. Jalasti, while more prudent in his desire to take his garrison archers as well, didn't seem fazed by the problem of what to do once they'd found the Old Man. Aida sighed.

Uratthurai was a pleasant place, rendered pleasant, Omar suspected, because everyone there knew that they were travelling with Jalasti. The market place was full, and the crew of the Blue Nymph was amazed to see the elephants which travelled on large ships from the port, as they slowly ambled in long lines through the port town.

"We could change this part of our journey and make it overland, on elephants," Jalasti offered with a perfectly straight face, as he watched Byrne and Ralf staring at the pachyderms.

Omar overheard and gave Jalasti a friendly clout over the head. "Get those country boats ready," he said, as he went to speak with Sinbad.

It had been decided that only Sinbad, Tishimi, and Byrne would travel with Aida and Jalasti to Mannar, the others remaining behind with the Blue Nymph.

Jalasti set off to make arrangements for the country boats they were to travel in, and then returned with three men who were willing to take them to Mannar. From Mannar, they would travel with Jalasti's archers in the ships which were on the island.

The voyage would be a short one, perhaps a day's sailing.

The sun beat down heavily. As noon drew closer, Jalasti called a halt.

"The men can't go on during the noon heat," he told Sinbad. "We shall pull into this small bay here and rest, have a meal perhaps."

They swung the boats into the bay and the boatmen beached the vessels. They immediately ran up the beach to a venerable old banyan that stood just beyond the sand and made obeisance, placing some food they had brought with them on a simple platform in a forked branch.

"Who is the god here?" Sinbad inquired.

Jalasti shrugged. "There are gods everywhere."

"It is the Black Prince," one of the boatmen said, overhearing.

"Who is the Black Prince?" Sinbad asked. They made their way to the shade of the trees. A small stream flowed out to the sea here, and vegetation grew thickly around it.

"He lives here. We always bring offerings for him, for he takes sacrifices if we don't," the sailor related.

"Another one like that, eh," Sinbad said, musingly.

They ate some food, and sat in the shade as the sun climbed past its zenith.

Finally, Jalasti stood up and brushed the sand from his robe. "Let's get moving."

Before any of them could move, however, a voice broke in. "Why leave so soon?" it asked.

Six weapons were drawn in the blink of an eye, the rasp of steel sounding like the angry buzzing of hornets.

A low chuckle came to their ears.

"Who is it?" Sinbad called out. The voice had come from the vegetation surrounding the stream, and all of them faced that way, naked weapons at the ready.

"Oh, don't let me inconvenience you," said the voice, and a man strolled out of the thick bush. There was no way he could have emerged from the dense jungle without crawling and twisting himself, so Sinbad was already suspecting him of being more than mortal before he noticed the lack of footprints on the sand over which the man passed.

He was black as night, not black as Aida was but in a more impossible way, an inhuman way. His neatly pointed beard was black as well, and he wore a red cloth around his waist.

"Who are you, and what do you want?" Sinbad demanded. Jalasti shook his head at him, but Sinbad didn't make the connection until the newcomer sauntered over to the banyan and took the food that the boatmen had just left as offering.

"Ooh, plantains," the Black Prince peeled one and began eating it.

He gave the boatmen a crocodile-ish smile. "You always know just what I want to eat," he said, graciously.

Sinbad shifted his scimitar in his hand slightly, and suddenly felt an extra weight at his side- and knew, with a sinking of his stomach, that Grachene had reappeared. Great, thanks, he thought, I really needed that possessed blade to show up again. He thought he heard an echo of a goddess' laughter, and then shook his head to clear it.

"What do you want?" Jalasti resheathed his blade, and was almost rolling his eyes as he spoke to the Black Prince.

"Come, come, Jalasti," the Black Prince said disapprovingly. "Is that the way to talk to me? You never leave offerings for me like these men do."

"Because I owe allegiance to one who is greater than you," Jalasti retorted.

The Black Prince sighed, openly rolling his eyes. "Is this about Allah again? I thought we'd agreed that an invisible all-powerful god who never appears is less important than the visible, regionally-powerful god who actually shows up."

Jalasti refused to answer.

"What do you want?" Sinbad repeated Jalasti's question. He had not sheathed his blade, and neither had Tishimi or Byrne.

The Black Prince sighed and looked with distaste at the exposed blades. "Please put those away, and then we can talk."

Jalasti shrugged. "Put em up, I suppose. He can't touch us here since the boatmen made the offering."

With reluctance, the Blue Nymph crew put their weapons away.

"Well, well, well," the Black Prince chortled with glee and while rubbing his hands. "What a nice day this is turning out to be. How nice of you all to…"

"Get to the point!" Sinbad snarled.

The Prince looked affronted. "What about the exchange of pleasantries?"

"Skip it," Jalasti barked.

"Oh, all right then. Long story short, I am going to take a sacrifice of you."

In a flash, Jalasti's sword was in his hand. "What do you mean? What treachery is this? We paid you tribute. Now you cannot touch us!"

At the sight of his blade emerging, Sinbad and his crew had once more drawn their weapons. Sinbad drew Grachene, not entirely willingly. The blade twitched in his hand as he faced the Black Prince.

The Black Prince remained unmoved. "That tribute is all well and good under normal circumstances."

"And why aren't these normal circumstances?" Sinbad demanded.

"You have two women with you. Unfortunately I will have to insist that they stay here with me, because we can't have them out at sea, can we?"

"This arrangement was good enough for you all these years," Jalasti growled.

"Ah, but you see, it was only one woman then," the Black Prince reminded. "Today I see two. So I shall have to keep them both."

"What can we do to change your mind?" Byrne interrupted.

"Oh, nothing. At least, nothing that you would be willing to do."

" IS THAT THE WAY TO TALK TO ME ? "

"What is it?" Jalasti demanded.

"It's a small errand," the Prince continued. "But it would take a day or two to accomplish. And we all know you don't have a day or two to spare."

"What do you mean, we don't have a day or two to spare?" Jalasti blurted out.

The Black Prince looked at him with well-simulated surprise. "Oh, don't you know? The Old Man of the Sea is going back to the seabed in two days' time. Taking with him everything he's managed to collect on this visit."

They drew to a side of the beach, leaving the boatmen sitting in awe at the Black Prince's feet. He was holding forth about the offerings he liked to receive.

"Can he hear us?" Tishimi hissed.

Jalasti shrugged. "Probably, but we don't really have a choice, do we?"

"We do, actually," Byrne put in, even as Sinbad and Aida were shaking their heads.

"What do you mean?" Aida asked.

"Your dagger, Sinbad," Byrne turned to his captain. "The, uh, special one."

Sinbad drew Grachene. He turned it hilt-first to the Scotsman, who held up his hands.

"No, no, you must do it," he argued. "But usually with those daggers you can make some sort of protection. At least a circle or something around us, to keep him from eavesdropping."

"Are you sure?" Sinbad was skeptical. He used the point of the dagger to trace a circle in the sand anyway.

"Isn't that a bit too cramped?" Jalasti began, doubtfully looking at the circle.

"Shut up and get inside it," Sinbad ordered.

They did, all standing uncomfortably close to each other.

"How are we going to defeat him?" Byrne whispered despite his assurances that the magic circle would make them inaudible.

"He controls the sea around here," Jalasti reminded them gloomily. "Besides, he can probably call on the Old Man of the Sea to help him out if he needs."

"We can possibly take him on…" Sinbad began, thinking fast. "But no, that won't do…well, we could…"

Tishimi cut him off. "Have you forgotten that he specifically said that the Old Man of the Sea will sink back down in two days' time? We don't have time to come up with a good plan and defeat him, *and* go on and collect Jalasti's archers, *and* defeat the Old Man of the Sea."

"So what's our alternative?" Sinbad raised an eyebrow.

Tishimi and Aida glanced at each other.

"You leave Tishimi and I here and go on to Mannar, and then collect the rest of the crew from Uratthurai. We complete the Black Prince's little errand and join you." Aida offered.

Jalasti spluttered. "We can't leave you here! This demon is crazy!"

"I can't leave a crew member behind," Sinbad declared.

Tishimi snorted. "If you don't leave me behind, we might not have time to defeat the Old Man of the Sea and get Rafi and Henri back!"

"Yes," Byrne added, "let's leave them and go on to collect the archers. Tishimi and Aida can take care of themselves, and even if they can't finish the challenge we can always rescue them on our way back to Uratthurai."

"We won't need any saving," Aida disagreed indignantly. "But apart from that, Byrne is right. Get a move on before the time is up!"

"All right then," Sinbad finally conceded. "Let's go tell the Black Prince."

They stepped out of the circle and turned towards the Black Prince, who, together with the boatmen, was looking at them with interest.

"Excellent choice," he beamed cheerfully. "We did enjoy your little ritual of the circle, and we were happy to follow your arguing and logic. By the way, Jalasti, I am neither a demon, nor am I crazy, as you so elegantly put it."

Everyone turned to look at Byrne. He merely shrugged.

"He is too a demon," Jalasti said under his breath, as they joined the boatmen in preparing to cast off.

"Stay safe," Sinbad commanded Aida and Tishimi. "If the quest gets too dangerous, stall for time until we can come help."

"No chance," Tishimi scoffed. "You just want a bit of the action for yourself."

The boats set off into the afternoon sun. Tishimi, Aida and the Black Prince watched them go. When they had disappeared into the heat haze, the Black Prince smiled at the women now under his command. "Now, about that errand…"

Aida wiped the sweat out of her eyes. She looked at the boat, then down the beach where, in the fast-gathering twilight, she could just make out the figure of the Black Prince, lounging on the sand.

"It's taken us so long to just fit this boat out," she grumbled to Tishimi.

"I only hope that's all that there is to it," her companion nodded.

"What do you mean?"

"He said once we'd fitted out the boat, we could row straight out to sea, didn't he?"

"Ye-es,"

"Well, then we could, according to him, easily collect the pearls from the oyster bank, couldn't we?"

Aida blinked. "That's what he said, yes."

Tishimi slammed her fist down on the side of the boat. "Why is it so easy? What's the catch?"

Aida jumped. "Uh, oysters? No, seriously. Do you think there is a catch? Maybe it's that pearl fishing isn't as easy as you think it is."

"And how hard is it?" Tishimi scoffed. "I know those who fish for pearls right across the ocean, from Nippon to the Gulf of Aden. Surely these pearls cannot be any harder to reach?"

"I don't know," Aida admitted, "but there are sharks. The sea takes sacrifices here."

"We can handle those." Tishimi was supremely confident in her own abilities.

They turned to the boat again, and soon it was ready, just as the last rays of a colorful sunset sank out of sight on the horizon.

"Demon!" Tishimi called, walking down the beach towards where they'd last seen the Black Prince.

Aida cringed a little.

Someone sighed right behind her, and she whipped around to see the Black Prince sitting, one leg cocked up, on the edge of the boat.

"I am a *god*, not a *demon*," he glared at them.

"Whatever. We've fixed the boat, and now we're heading out to those pearl banks," Tishimi said, insolently.

"In the dark?" the Black Prince asked. "Sharks are around. I wouldn't want anything happening to you."

"You said that we have only two days before the Old Man of the Sea disappears. We're just making use of every moment we have." Tishimi was unsmiling, and unwavering in the way that she looked straight at the Black Prince.

The Black Prince turned away slightly and covered his smile.

Tishimi and Aida watched him, bemused.

"Two days? Oh dear, did I say two days?" he waved a hand in the air. "How remiss of me. You actually have till noon tomorrow."

Aida had never seen someone move so quickly. One moment Tishimi had been motionless, standing a little away from her on the beach, and the next she had landed like a springing tiger on the Black Prince, knocking him to the ground and pinning him down with one hand. Her other hand held her katana at the demon's throat.

"What do you mean, noon tomorrow?" she shouted.

The Black Prince looked completely unruffled, and shrugged his shoulders suddenly and violently. Besides momentarily causing Tishimi to lose her grip on his robe, he changed nothing by his movement. Her blade remained steady at his throat.

The Black Prince, however, seemed distressed. His eyes grew wide and rolled in all directions, as if seeking an escape. He started hyperventilating.

"Aida, get some water," Tishimi called over her shoulder.

She moved back, allowing the demon to sit up, but keeping her sword at his throat all the while. He calmed down with the drink of water.

"Why can't I move?" he whined.

"Maybe because I'm literally holding you down?"

"No, it's…" his eyes landed on the katana. "It's this blade! You have a magic blade!" He began writhing and wailing.

"Is it magic?" Aida asked, curiously.

Tishimi ignored her. "Look, demon, if you want to take your head with you when you go, you've got to clean up this mess you've dumped us in."

"I can't," the Black Prince wailed. "He made me do it!"

"Who, the Old Man of the Sea?" Aida queried.

At the name, the Black Prince writhed and squealed more. "Not him," he said at last, "his lieutenant!"

"Another one to deal with?" Aida frowned.

"Let's deal with him when we get to him," Tishimi turned her attention back to the Black Prince. "Sort this out, now." She jabbed him with her katana.

"I can't! He will come back and kill me!"

"Fine. Then at least do something to even out our odds."

The demon squirmed. "N-never!"

Tishimi shifted her katana to her other hand, keeping it at his throat, and held out her hand. "Aida, give me the other weapon."

Aida's look of utter confusion went unnoticed by the demon, who was more focused on Tishimi's next words. "The magical weapon that separates demons' spirits from their bodies." .

The Black Prince blanched. "Let me go, let me go!" he begged. "I'll give you twenty-four hours, I'll put you back at noon today. That's all I can do, please let me go!"

Tishimi looked at Aida. "What do you think?"

Aida nodded. "We can make that work."

Sinbad stretched, yawning widely. He opened his eyes, and then started, setting the boat rocking.

"Why didn't anyone wake me up? Why have I slept an entire day away?"

The boatmen were nowhere in sight.

Byrne and Jalasti turned strained eyes upon him. "You didn't sleep an entire day," Byrne corrected.

"Then how is it noon? We left the Black Prince's beach in the afternoon, and we've been travelling since." Sinbad drew his scimitar with a curse, and turned on Jalasti. "You've lied to us, and led us astray! You said it would take until nightfall to reach your fort! It is now half a day later!"

Jalasti drew his own sword. "You sorcerer! You have caused this...this weird situation!"

Byrne looked to the heavens, and then placed a hand on each of the sword's flats. He shoved them away. "Look, both of you!" he rapped out. "This is the work of the Old Man of the Sea. There's no point in us becoming divided now."

"What even happened?!" Sinbad roared.

"Right, so you were asleep and then the sun started setting, and just after it had set, something happened. It was as if we saw the sunset in reverse, within a few minutes. And now it's noon again." Byrne recounted.

Sinbad narrowed his eyes. "What do you mean, noon again?"

Byrne held out his hands palms out. "Unless, of course, it's noon tomorrow."

"The sunset was in reverse," Jalasti pointed out.

"But how?" Sinbad scratched his head.

"You're the one with a magic dagger," Jalasti said, sulkily. "You're the one who knows all about sorcery."

"This is not my work," Sinbad replied, angrily.

Things looked fair to become another argument, when Byrne shouted, "Land ho!"

"My fort," smiled Jalasti, proudly.

"Where are the boatmen?" Sinbad inquired.

"They jumped overboard when the sun rose again," Byrne explained. "Said they'd rather lose their boats than be with those who crossed the Black Prince."

Sinbad scowled. "What was that you said about a magnetic fort?"

"It won't work on this boat, because it's sewn, but once we get a bit closer you'll have to wrap up your blades." Jalasti cautioned.

"Wrap up our blades?" Sinbad didn't believe his ears. "How will we fight then?"

"No, no, there are these...amulets...that you can attach to your pommel. They counteract the force of the fort. But those are there in the fort itself, so I can't give them to you until we land."

Sinbad stared at Jalasti, eyes narrowed.

"Don't believe me? Watch this." Jalasti pulled out a small dagger and set it in the prow.

"Keep your weapons under some cloth," he instructed, "unless of course you don't mind watching them go with the dagger."

Reluctantly, Sinbad and Byrne complied. Sinbad kept a firm grip on his swords under the cloth.

As they approached the fort, the dagger in the prow twitched and quivered. Then, with a quick motion, it flew from the prow across the waves.

Sinbad's eyes bulged.

The next moment, his and Byrne's weapons started quivering violently, even under their layers of cloth.

"We've got to get out of the force-field," Jalasti began rowing.

Neither Byrne or Sinbad were able to help him, having both hands full with keeping their weapons under control.

Eventually, they drew closer to the island, and the weapons vibrated less and less. Finally they stopped quivering and remained still. Sinbad immediately snatched his scimitar out, holding it ready. The boat drew to a halt at a pier, which was busy with a crowd of people.

"My lord!" a man called, standing to receive Jalasti as he clambered out of the boat. Sinbad and Byrne followed.

"We need archers," Jalasti ordered. "And amulets for these men's weapons."

"Will you be embarking immediately?" the man inquired, deferentially.

"After a meal. Have them prepare one in the fort."

The man turned and gave orders to others. Jalasti turned to Sinbad and Byrne. "Let's go talk to the archers, and let them know the plan."

"Do you have a vessel that we could use to return to Uratthurai in?" Byrne asked. "We could shave off some of the time we took if we had a faster vessel."

Jalasti looked at him, oddly. Byrne was slightly disquieted by the look, but when he glanced to Sinbad to see if he had noticed, the captain was staring about him with frank interest, and apparently had not seen the look. "Yes, we can use one of my ships." Jalasti said, leading the way towards the side of the towering metal fort.

It was well after nightfall when the ship, laden with Jalasti's archers, came into sight of the harbour at Uraththurai.

"We have some time," Jalasti remarked. "I don't think we needed to return in such a hurry as we did."

"The sooner we do this, the better," Sinbad said. "The Black Prince said two days, which probably means that now we have something like a day and a half left."

"But what about that weird time thing that happened?" Byrne asked. "Did that take away another half-day?"

"In that case, we have only a day left. We'll have to get to work." Sinbad peered anxiously into the dark harbour to see the Blue Nymph.

"Sinbad!" someone whispered, in a low rumbling voice that rolled across the water like thunder.

"Ralf!" Sinbad hissed back, and the next moment the prow of the Blue Nymph loomed up in the water.

Jalasti motioned to his bo'sun to stop the rowers, and the sewn ship pulled up alongside the Blue Nymph. Sinbad was across the bows in a flash, relieved to be back on his familiar ship again.

"What happens now?" Jalasti asked. "Shall we leave at first light?"

"A couple of hours of sleep would do you good," Ralf agreed.

"I don't think we should waste any time at all," Byrne objected. "I have an uneasy feeling about this whole situation, and the sooner we get Tishimi, Rafi and Henri back, the better I will feel."

"I wonder how Aida and Tishimi are getting on," Jalasti mused.

"Byrne is right," Sinbad concurred. "It doesn't make sense for us to waste any time. Let's head out to sea."

"What about Tishimi and Aida?" Ralf glanced about. "Where are they?"

In a few terse sentences, Sinbad brought him up to date.

The Norseman scowled. "I don't like the thought of leaving them to handle things. Although I know Tishimi at least is very capable of protecting herself."

"But as we came back, we passed the area where the Black Prince is said to be, and we saw no sight of them." Jalasti added. "We thought it best to return here and join forces with you."

"So we have two options," Omar, the first mate, had silently joined them and spoke now for the first time. "One is to return along the coast and attempt to find Tishimi and Aida. The other is to head straight out to sea and confront the Old Man of the Sea."

"Well, what do you think is best?" Jalasti asked.

Omar turned to Sinbad. "This is your decision, I think." They all looked at Sinbad.

He frowned, thinking hard. He would have to make a decision soon, for even as they stood on the deck, the night was getting darker. Soon the sky would begin to lighten in the east. The crews watched him, wondering what was going through his mind.

Eventually, Sinbad looked up. "We head out to sea."

"What about Tishimi and Aida?" Byrne asked.

Sinbad turned to Jalasti. "Can we take your archers on board the Blue Nymph?"

Jalasti looked dubiously at the archers, standing on the deck of the sewn ship. "I suppose it would be all right, since it's probably a short voyage."

"Then can we ask your bo'sun to head back along the coast to the Black Prince's area? They can search for Aida and Tishimi. But the rest of us had better head out to find the Old Man of the Sea without delay."

Jalasti acquiesced. He turned and gave some orders to his men. The archers leapt aboard, and the sewn ship slowly moved away, the rowers picking up pace as they headed towards the mouth of the harbor.

Omar bellowed orders and the Blue Nymph sprang into activity in the silent harbor. The archers stood aside on the deck as the crew ran about, readying the ship for its voyage and battle.

The first gleams of a new day were streaking the sky behind them as the Blue Nymph moved slowly out into the open sea, already beginning to be speckled with the fishermen's catamarans, and then her sky-blue sails caught the morning breeze and billowed out.

Night had just fallen when Aida and Tishimi realized that something was wrong. The sea in front of them looked wrong. Here, miles out from the land, the sea ought to have been deeper, but Tishimi could reach the bottom, or at least, some sort of surface with the end of her katana.

"Stop rowing," she told Aida, who was only too glad to rest her aching arms. The boat bobbed lazily on the sea, and they looked around them.

"Why is the sea so shallow here?" Tishimi asked, worried.

"Oh," said Aida, "I think these are the pearl banks."

Tishimi looked over the edge of the boat. "I don't see any pearls."

"I have never been here before," Aida confessed, "but I've heard that the pearl divers bring their boats here and dive beyond these shallows."

"Paddle a little more, so I can see," Tishimi requested, and sure enough, as the boat slid forwards, the floor of the ocean dropped away again.

"Now we've got to figure out how to dive for those pearls," Aida pondered.

"All right." Tishimi unbuckled her sword belt. She shed her outer cloak of black silk. "I'm going to dive."

"What about sharks?" Aida asked.

"You keep a look out here."

"I could dive too."

"Well, maybe once I come up we'll switch places. But you would be of more use up here with your arrows, just in case a shark or two appears."

With a splash, Tishimi went overboard. The boat rocked with the sudden

"WHY IS THE SEA SO SHALLOW HERE?"

shift of weight, and then the ripples closed, and Aida was alone under the barely-visible moon. The sea spread out on either side of her, empty and peaceful.

Tishimi broke the surface a moment later. "I can hardly see anything down there."

"Do you think we ought to wait till morning?"

"No, we'll have even less time then. We've got to find these pearls and get them back to the Black Prince before we can find the others and the Old Man of the Sea."

"Well, you stay up in the boat and I'll dive," Aida unslung her bow.

Tishimi shook her head decisively and dived again.

Half an hour later, Aida had to help her struggle back into the boat. Her strength was almost completely gone, and she lay in a sodden heap at the bottom of the boat for a while, regaining her breath. Repeated dives to the bottom had availed nothing, and she had been forced each time to surface empty-handed.

"I don't think diving for pearls is as easy as the Black Prince made it sound," Aida stated once Tishimi's breathing had evened out.

"But we don't have a choice, do we?" Tishimi snapped, sitting up. "Unless, of course, you're actually happy that we're getting delayed, and that the Old Man of the Sea will be able to disappear with Rafi and Henri."

Aida looked wounded. "Tishimi! Do you really still think that?"

"I don't know what to think."

"I don't know what else I can say to prove my innocence. So you're just going to have to decide whether or not to trust me. Only it's a little late in the day to decide you don't trust me."

"Well, if you are actually innocent, then you would dive and look for the pearls!" Tishimi accused.

"You're the one who told me to stay in the boat," Aida reminded her, coldly.

She had just let herself over the side of the boat into the water when Tishimi reached out and grabbed her arm.

"Get back in," she ordered.

Aida fought off her grip. "What the devil? Do you want me to dive or not?"

But Tishimi wasn't looking at her. Her eyes were fixed on a point behind Aida. Aida turned to look, and her blood ran cold. Through the starlit night, a triangular object swam slowly towards them. Even as she looked, other triangles approached the first and swam in.

With one fluid movement, displaying an athleticism worthy of her boat-mate, Aida twisted her body out of the water and over the side of the boat, almost capsizing it in the process. Tishimi drew her sword, and Aida hastily dried her hands before nocking an arrow on her bow.

They watched the fins approach them in silence. The nearest one was a yard away when there was a sudden, bone-jarring thud and the boat flopped in the water.

Both women lost their balance, luckily remaining in the boat.

"Something's trying to capsize us," Aida breathed.

"They've surrounded us," Tishimi groaned, as she looked around. Triangular fins circled the boat. As Aida looked, she felt something was strange about the order in which the fins were placed- almost as if the sharks were swimming in formation, each shark a specific distance from the next.

"Something's not right," she muttered, and Tishimi nodded. They drew closer to each other, backs to each other and their weapons ready.

The fins moved together, as one.

"Why are they so coordinated?" Aida puzzled, just as one fin reared up in the air, followed by another, and another, and another.

"Oh, *damn*," Tishimi stared upwards as the monstrous head of a sea-serpent rose up above them, blotting out the stars.

"We may reenter the force-field again," Jalasti told everyone, "so I would advise you to put these amulets on your weapons."

"What is that?" Omar was suspicious.

"We had them on our weapons coming out," Byrne said, "and they do protect the weapons from the magnetic pull."

Omar looked unconvinced, but as Sinbad repeated Jalasti's suggestion as an order, he shrugged and took one of the amulets that Jalasti offered. Across the ship, the men of Sinbad's crew were fitting the small stone amulets onto their weapons with the cord attached.

Byrne began telling Omar about the magnetic fort, which he had seen proof of, and they wandered off across the deck. The Blue Nymph was well under way, and the morning sun had just begun getting hotter.

"By my calculations, we have one hour more before we reach those sandbars the sailors told me about," Omar told Sinbad, as they reached the tiller.

"And were the sailors certain that we would meet the Old Man of the Sea there?" Sinbad asked.

"Yes, they were very anxious to tell me not to head anywhere near this direction. In fact, only one old man with one eye was able to tell me the exact location. He'd lost the eye in a fight with the Old Man of the Sea, I was told."

"Hmm." Sinbad gazed at the horizon.

"That gives us half a day at the very least to fight the Old Man of the Sea and get Rafi and Henri back," Omar calculated.

"Assuming the Black Prince didn't lie to us," Sinbad added.

Byrne nodded. "I still think it was strange, how the day skipped like that. Some magic is underfoot here, and I don't like it."

Sinbad gave a short, sardonic laugh. "We'll be lucky if that's the only magic we face on this voyage. Something tells me that the Old Man of the Sea has a few tricks left up his sleeve."

*SO GLAD TO MEET YOU AGAIN,* the sea-serpent greeted them, showing all of its three rows of needle-sharp teeth in a pointy grin.

Tishimi felt disoriented. Beside her, Aida was staring up at the monster, her mouth open.

*I DON'T SUPPOSE YOU REMEMBER ME,* the serpent went on. *I ONLY SPOKE TO SINBAD.*

Tishimi's brain started working again. "You're the Old Man of the Sea," she spat, lifting her blade.

*I HAVE BEEN CALLED THAT, YES,* the serpent admitted. *BUT THIS IS NOT MY TRUE FORM. I WOULDN'T WANT YOU THINKING THAT I USUALLY LOOK LIKE THIS! OH NO, I TAKE THIS FORM TO SCARE THE LOCALS. FISHERMEN AND SO ON, YOU KNOW.*

"What do you want?" Aida's voice was trembling.

The serpent laughed. *NOTHING FROM YOU, MY DEARS. I AM WAITING FOR MY SERVANT TO BRING THE OTHERS TO ME.*

"What servant?" Tishimi asked. "What others?" Aida echoed in the same instant.

The serpent seemed to find this amusing, and laughed even harder. As it laughed, its body quivered and shook, the tremors spreading from the upraised portion of its body to the many triangular fins that lay around the boat. The boat began rocking.

*YOU HAVE ALREADY MET MY SERVANT. AND AS FOR THE OTHERS— WHY, THEY ARE YOUR CREWMATES. I'VE ALREADY GOT TWO WITH ME, AND EVEN AS WE SPEAK, THE OTHERS ARE ON THEIR WAY TO JOIN US.*

"Has the Black Prince tricked them, then?" Tishimi inquired angrily.

"We already know that the Black Prince is your servant," Aida declared. "We aren't quite as dumb as you think we are."

The serpent stopped laughing, and wearing an evil grin, it brought its head down so it was just above the boat. Aida and Tishimi had to crane their necks backward to see it.

*EVERYBODY KNOWS THAT THE BLACK PRINCE IS MY SERVANT. NO, I'M TALKING ABOUT JALASTI.*

"Almost there," Omar called. "Get ready for any eventualities."

He took over the tiller as Sinbad strode among the crew and the archers, checking weapons and encouraging the men.

Neither of them noticed Jalasti furtively glancing at the horizon.

Sinbad hit a snag when he asked to see the archers' weapons. They refused to take orders from him, claiming that Jalasti was the only one who had the authority to give them orders.

"Jalasti!" Sinbad bellowed. "Check your archers' weapons, and I want them to answer to me, at least during battle."

"They might not like to."

Sinbad scowled. "In battle, we cannot afford to have two commanders. I will be the commander, and I want to have my every order obeyed instantly, without these men looking for you and double-checking all my commands."

"And what makes you more qualified to be commander?"

"This is my ship!"

For a moment, it seemed as if a repeat of their earlier argument would break out. Then Jalasti heaved a sigh.

"Fine." He turned to his men and spoke briefly to them.

Sinbad stuck his chin out and watched him. "I will be in charge for the rest of this voyage."

Jalasti rolled his eyes but walked away to the other side of the deck without replying.

Tishimi awoke with a start. She and Aida were curled together in the bottom of the boat. She peered over the side of the boat, and the sea lay calm and smooth in the mid-morning sun. Not a fin broke its surface, but in the nightmare morning they had just spent, she and Aida knew better than to assume that the sea-serpent had left.

Ever since hearing of her employer's treachery, Aida had had only one thought, to warn the Blue Nymph. Tishimi too had felt that was the one of the only things they could do; the other being killing the Old Man of the Sea themselves. Being Tishimi, she immediately tried out the latter plan, but the sea-serpent had proved too much for them.

Finally, battered and bruised, they had decided to row out and warn the Blue Nymph only to discover that the sea-serpent wasn't about to let that happen. Coils and coils of his body had wrapped around the boat, so that it stayed perfectly stationary. Tishimi's katana had left its mark on the enormous scaly body, but even so, even impregnated with the chi of her father, it had been unable to do more than leave a nasty but non-mortal cut on the sea-serpent.

As a last resort, driven to desperation, Tishimi threw herself overboard and began swimming but to no avail. She was soon snatched up and thrown back in by the tip of the monster's tail. Exhausted and demoralized, the two girls fell asleep at last, just as the sun was rising.

Tishimi had not slept well, waking every time a small noise reached her ears. She didn't wonder why she had woken again until she noticed the faint speck on the horizon. She watched it approach, infinitesimally slowly, until it was near enough for her to see the blueness of its sails against the blue of the clear, clean sky.

"Aida!" she hissed, shaking her companion.

"Wassa matter?" Aida sleepily rubbed her face and winced when she touched a bruise.

"The Blue Nymph is here."

Aida sprang up. "No!" she cried, in dismay.

"Shush!" Tishimi yanked her back down. "How can we warn them without the serpent noticing?"

"I don't know," Aida answered wearily.

They sat in silence, watching the ship draw nearer.

Suddenly, Tishimi's gaze fell on Aida's quiver of arrows. She snatched them up.

"Shoot this out!" she said, excitedly. "We can roll a message around the body. Henri used to do so whenever he had to get a message through to us."

Aida looked doubtful, but Tishimi gave her no chance to refused. She asked Aida for a strip of material from her under-shift, and, laying the light-colored cloth out on the bench, she cut her finger with her knife.

"What are you going to write?" Aida peered over Tishimi's shoulder.

"I don't have much room, J traitor, maybe?" She scrawled on the cloth with her blood as she did so.

"I hope they'll understand it."

Tishimi finished, and quickly rolled the strip up round an arrow one-handed, holding the bleeding hand away from the message cloth.

"Can you shoot this at the Blue Nymph, Aida?"

"The cloth is going to change the weight of the arrow and it won't leave the bow smoothly, so I'll have to mmmm..." her voice trailed off as she squinted at the Blue Nymph.

She stood up, nocked the message arrow to the bow. She sighted, changed the angle of the bow, and imagined the trajectory and then released it. The arrow went soaring up into the sky.

Neither of them breathed as they watched it as far as possible, and then their eyes traced the expected trajectory.

They could only hope that the Blue Nymph had gotten their message.

"There's a boat," Haroun called out. "Two people in it. One is standing up... now sitting down."

"Who are they?" Omar yelled up. "Friend or foe?"

"I can't see that much," Haroun replied. "I suppose we'll find out soon enough."

"Should we head towards the boat?" Omar asked Sinbad.

Sinbad thought for a moment. "All right." Omar swung the tiller a few degrees to the left.

"What are they doing now?" he shouted to Haroun.

"I can't see, they're crouching down. Oh, one's standing up and doing something. I can't quite see what but it looks very familiar. Now they're both standing and looking towards us, I think... it was an arrow! They fired an arrow..?"

Haroun's last words were chopped off by the thunk of an arrow that impaled itself in the wood between Sinbad's feet.

He stooped down, and peeled off the strip of cloth.

Everyone crowded around to see what it was.

"Who sent it?" Ralf asked.

"Those people in the boat, whoever they are," Byrne said.

"What does it say?" Jalasti asked.

Sinbad unrolled the cloth. "I...trailer," he read, slowly.

"What?" Byrne asked confused.

"I...oh wait, that's a t... I traitor," Sinbad corrected himself.

"What on earth does that mean?" Omar scratched his beard.

"I, traitor? Do they mean that they are traitors?" Ralf shook his head.

Sinbad repeated the words to himself, holding the cloth loosely in his hand. He felt some half-submerged thought nagging him at the back of his mind. He looked up, and his eyes met Jalasti's. Jalasti smiled mockingly, and suddenly light dawned in Sinbad's mind.

"J- traitor," he roared, throwing himself at Jalasti.

His crew, taken completely by surprise, failed to react for a few precious seconds; seconds in which the whole company of archers nocked arrows to their bows and covered all the Blue Nymph men.

Jalasti adroitly sidestepped Sinbad's charge, and when Sinbad pivoted, drawing his scimitar, it was just in time to meet Jalasti's drawn sword.

Sinbad hacked down…and shouted in pain, as his sword met the same force-field he had encountered the first time he tried to kill Jalasti.

"I knew you were in league with the Old Man of the Sea," Sinbad snarled, as he held his sword ready to swing again.

"But why did you let your guard down, then?" Jalasti smiled.

Sinbad swung again, and again had his arm jarred by the force-field. He almost dropped his scimitar. Omar had recovered enough to draw his sword, and he was about to step forward when one of the archers warned, "The first man to move gets an arrow in his throat!".

None of the archers saw Haroun, however, who had climbed around the rigging to get to the deck behind them. With their backs to him, none of them saw him as he sprang at the rearmost one, tackling him to the deck. Then he drew his dagger and was about to stab another archer when the watching crew saw his hand stop in its arc and then heard his cry of pain and alarm.

"Another force-field?" Byrne wondered aloud.

Jalasti smirked. "You let your guard down, *and* you let me tie amulets to all your weapons," he said, mockingly.

There was a collective gasp from the crew as they realized what had happened.

Ralf tried to tear the amulet away from his axe, but it wouldn't budge.

"I don't suppose you will be much of a threat if I turn my back on you now," Jalasti chuckled and turned around to face the sea.

"O great one, I have returned, bringing you these offerings," he cried out, in a loud voice.

Aida and Tishimi watched helplessly as the triangular fins reappeared. Some remained around the boat, but the others snaked out across the sea to the Blue Nymph. The fins around the boat soon contracted, and they felt the serpent's tail wrapping around it. It drew the boat towards the ship in its wake.

The sea-serpent reared its head.

*HELLO, MY LOYAL SERVANT, AND HELLO, SINBAD.*

Sinbad raged.

*TOSS THEM IN, JALASTI, AND I'LL BE ON MY WAY. I'M IN A HURRY TO GO BACK DOWN.*

The layers of teeth gleamed horridly in the dark cavernous mouth as the sea-serpent swayed slightly above the Blue Nymph.

Jalasti turned to Sinbad. "You heard him. You can, of course, jump in of your own accord?"

Sinbad's only reply was to lunge at Jalasti again.

*SOMEONE SEEMS RELUCTANT TO JOIN ME,* the se-serpent boomed.

Ralf took a step forward, and the archer's threat proved to not be vain. An arrow sliced past his body, nicking his arm.

"That was a warning shot," the archer called, but his voice was not quite steady and Byrne suspected something awry. From the look of the archers, they had not expected the appearance of the sea-serpent.

*YOUR CREWMATES ARE ALREADY WITH ME,* the sea-serpent declared. The crew on board the Blue Nymph saw Aida and Tishimi in the boat. Haroun called out and pointed, and, bobbing on the water, they saw Rafi and Henri.

*COME JOIN THEM,* the serpent encouraged.

Jalasti took a step towards Sinbad.

Sinbad was torn for a moment. By going in, he could perhaps save his crewmates, or at the very least, they would be together for the next great adventure.

Omar sensed his thoughts. "Don't be stupid, Sinbad, he's going to kill us!"

Sinbad snapped back into reality. His mind went into overdrive. If he could only get rid of Jalasti, the rest of them could do something. But not with those archers.

At that moment, Tishimi drew her katana and began hacking at whatever part of the sea-serpent's body she could reach. Aida stood up in the boat and began shouting.

"Aida?" an archer looked over the side of the ship.

"Jalasti has betrayed everyone!" she called. "The men who were lost in Tyndis harbour, this monster took them! Yet Jalasti works for him!"

"My brother was lost in Tyndis," said of the archers.

"Then help us get these amulets off!" Byrne cried, seeing which way they were hesitating.

Jalasti realized the archers' support would not be forthcoming, and turned to face Sinbad.

Sinbad glanced down at his scimitar, and then flung it aside. It clattered on the deck, and Jalasti's eyes just had time to widen in fear before Sinbad hit his legs in a flying tackle and pushed him over the side.

Then they all turned their efforts on the sea-serpent. Weakened as it was by the wounds from Tishimi's katana, and running out of time on the surface, it gave way rapidly.

*YOU WILL NOT WIN EVERYTHING. I WILL TAKE MY SACRIFICE WITH ME.*

Tishimi gasped. She and Aida glanced at each other, and then, both understanding, rowed with all the power they could towards the unconscious bodies of Rafi and Henri.

The sounds of the battle were deafening, with the sea-serpent roaring directly above them, but they made it. They dragged Rafi and Henri into the boat, and then began rowing back.

"We have to get clear before he goes under," Tishimi gasped.

Aida didn't bother replying, but bent to the task of rowing.

They were almost at the ship, and the sea-serpent had slid very low in the water, when its tail wrapped around the boat.

It slapped Tishimi against the side, where she lay stunned. Aida continuing rowing but to no avail against the force of the serpent.

Sinbad rushed to the side of the ship, and took in what was happening in a glance. He felt a weight at his side. Without looking, he knew what it was, and with a flying leap he landed in the water near the boat.

Drawing Grachene, he sank the blade to the hilt in the tail of the serpent.

Two minutes later, everything was over, and the Blue Nymph once more the only thing breaking the calm surface of the sea.

They sailed back to Uraththurai, to leave the archers and Aida behind. As the Blue Nymph sailed into the afternoon sky, Tishimi looked at Aida.

"Well, maybe I was wrong," she said. "Maybe you aren't an agent of the Old Man of the Sea after all."

# The End

# The Challenge of Writing

I have always enjoyed pulp fiction, though I wasn't specifically aware of it as a genre. The inspiration to write pulp came to me only after years of trying (and failing miserably) to write 'Literature' (with a capital L). Since I flatter myself that I can, at least, tell a story, I gave up completely on my delusions of literary grandeur and decided to write stories that people would enjoy. I just spent three years researching maritime violence in a similar time period- if you have enough obscure knowledge you will be able to see the specific instances in the story. So as soon as Captain Ron suggested Sinbad as my maiden Airship 27 venture, I leapt at the chance. In fact, it was while writing this story that I realized just how much I didn't know, and it also relit my enthusiasm for the research I had been doing. Writing the story has been a rather fun process- thinking of the plot has whiled away many boring hours in the bus and bathroom, and getting back into the research has really helped my other writing. Since the last time I wrote about a similar situation was at university, focusing on this story highlighted the little gaps that you can easily gloss over when writing a scholarly paper- like what exactly would the characters have worn? Obviously the canonical characters are already dressed, thank goodness, but the new minor characters had to be.

**TERRY WIJESURIYA** is a student of history, who seems to spend her whole life writing in different forms. She reads not wisely nor too well, but certainly widely. She is inspired by whatever book she read last, but has a special soft spot in her heart for Orientalist swashbucklers like *Lost Horizon*. In her spare time she runs a sporadic fan blog for J.T. Edson's floating outfit series (theysabelkid.wordpress.com). Her dream is to be a chain-smoking, hard-drinking pulp fiction author, which would be more likely to come true if she wasn't a teetotaler who never smokes.

# THE HITTITE SWORD GOD
by J. Walt Layne

On the night of the troubled moon the Blue Nymph was moored off Mersin, Akdeiz in the shadow of Anatolia. Ten days out of the Greek spice market at Agia Roumeli the crew was doing brisk trade from port to port in the Mediterranean. They'd put to sea late from the night bazaar at Tisan and the morning watch had come on under a crimson sky. Through the long afternoon the dark clouds gave the impression of night in the lands of perpetual sun and the crew brought their ship into Yeni harbor with a weather eye for a place to lay in for the night.

The Sahil Pazari market teemed with merchants and customers buying spices, cloth, silver and gold. Some men were looking for wives, other men were looking for slaves. Others were looking to shanghai boys and youths into lives of unintentional adventure or worse.

The Captain of the Blue Nymph, Sinbad Al Ari, a roguishly handsome, six foot tall thirty-year-old had taken the core crew ashore to trade and resupply. Haroun, the lookout had been left in charge of the few remaining crew and left with orders to make repairs and scrub down every surface from stem to stern.

Ashore Omar had headed to the local hostel in search of stout young men of strong courage who might be interested in going to sea. Henri and Ralf sought to resupply their store of ale and wines and seek diversion. They'd immediately gone off in the direction of a bawdy sounding crowd. Tishimi perused the bazaar, speaking with a basket weaver, a tea merchant and a haggard looking fellow who ran the brazier.

Sometime later Rafi, accompanied by a boy who carried the doctor's supplies in a large basket upon his head meandered toward the end of the bazaar. Rafi noticed Tishimi speaking with the paper merchant and stared past her at a very pregnant woman who shrieked and stumbled her way out of the tent of the oil seller.

At first glance he thought the woman was accompanied by a hag dressed in a red rag dress. He watched the woman stammer and carry on as the crowded square parted to give her a very wide berth as she lurched this way and that as if she were going to tumble and grind in on her face. She walked headlong into

Ralf who turned on her, raising a fist.

"No, you must not." The wine merchant stayed the mountainous Viking's hand. "She is cursed. The Al Karisi is upon her."

"Al Karisi? Albis? Have you been sampling the new wines then?" Ralf asked, shaking free of the man's small but wiry grip.

A Hebrew woman in the crowd nodded her agreement as Ralf's raised voice had drawn the attention of Rafi and Tishimi and they approached quietly. "The Albis are terrible wicked things. They prey on women with child, infants and the peuperant. They feed on the liver."

Rafi stayed Ralf with an arm. He blinked and shook his head. The hag in the rag dress was there and gone. As he looked away again, the hag was in his periphery, tormenting the pregnant woman. When he looked at the pitiful sight directly, he could not see the hag, only her tortured victim.

The Hebrew woman's husband was suddenly there and grabbed her by the arm, "Sari, get home and take the children."

He gave the Viking and the lady Samurai distrustful looks, and the woman Sari took a small boy and girl by the hand and hurried them away at her husband's behest.

The cursed woman now stood at the center of the bazaar shrieking and convulsing. Her terrifying cries in Farsi, Turkic and another tongue, Nisili unknown to any in the bazaar.

Rafi went to the woman despite Tishimi trying to dissuade him. He tried to guide her to a place to sit, but she thrashed and slapped him across the face. "Stop that, now!" He said firmly and she wailed.

The wine merchant interceded, "You cannot help her, the Al Karisi has chosen her. A stake must be driven through the demon's heart, or it will eventually tire this woman to sleep and take her liver and the liver of her unborn."

As Rafi began to question the man, he heard the familiar cantankerous and borderline belligerent banter of Omar approaching from behind.

"What in the Jinn of Samara's harem is going on?" He stopped gape mouthed as the contorted woman walked back bent, pregnant belly skyward, cursing in Aramaic.

Sinbad arrived just as the girl ran out of the bazaar. He shook a goatskin pouch and turned out a few rubies into his hand and gripped them tight, shaking his fist in victory, "Thanks to Omar, I was able to trade all of the henna cloth to the dressmakers and an Akkadian prince will come to the ship later to purchase all of the juniper berries. They dry roast them to make something called Pep'per." He put the rubies back into the pouch and stuffed it into his sash.

In his midst the pregnant woman shrieked and for the briefest moment he saw the hag clawing at her. As he made eye contact the visage of the hag was transformed into the most appealing seductress his eyes had ever beheld. The woman screamed and their eye contact was broken.

Sinbad cleared his vision and the hag was gone, but her tormented victim remained "I have seen this, but it confounds me. It's not a curse as I understand them, having been cursed more than once and had to find cure and counter to more than one." Sinbad offered but no one could take their eyes off the disturbed woman.

"The Albis, an Al Karisi is upon her. It will kill her and her child if we don't do something." Tishimi warned.

The wailing intensified and the tormented woman began turning over tables. Screaming and thrashing about as she went, crying out to some unseen force. Her beckoning, begging cries for relief followed by wailing again in some unknown tongue.

As she began smashing blown glassware and slinging pottery Rafi again went to the woman calling to his friends, "Help me we have to immobilize her so she can't harm anyone, her unborn child included."

Ralf moved in behind the woman and was about to grab her when she turned with unnatural speed, darted between him and the unsuspecting Henri and ducked into the carpet seller's tent.

"She's bewitched. This is madness." Henri exclaimed as he turned and headed toward the tent, following Ralf and Rafi. Sinbad and Omar looked on in amusement.

The boy with the basket still resting upon his head spoke up, "It is not just the Albis, the Zaar has been upon her for months now. Not like this, but at least once in a fortnight it brings her to these fits. She drove her husband mad with the wailing and he has left his house to live among the urchins."

"The Zaar is just an opportunistic Jinn on the wind. A Zaar Ma'ma and Baba can hold a Giri and rid her of it." He said, and turned toward the sounds of her chaos, "Where is her house?" Sinbad demanded.

The boy looked up at the captain from beneath his basket and started to raise a finger when the wailing woman burst forth from the carpet seller's tent, riding a flying prayer rug. She let go a blood curdling scream and leaned forward on her rug, flying straight for the boy.

Sinbad seized the boy and his basket, pulling him out of the way as the woman on her rug shot past missing by a mere whisker.

"Come ashore he says, it will be fun he says," Omar grouched just before the woman bowled him over, causing him to turn over his own heavy parcel of supplies.

As she circuited the tables, the carpet was erratic under her convulsions. She turned toward the paper merchant's tables and picked up speed. As she shot past Tishimi the samurai shot out a short snapping punch that connected at the base of the woman's skull.

The woman collapsed on the prayer rug, and it slowed to a stop, coming to rest at Rafi's feet.

"Quickly, bind her hands and feet. She will not be unconscious for long, and we may not have another chance." Sinbad ordered, unwinding a cord from the scabbard of his scimitar.

They bound the woman and Rafi did his best to make her comfortable as she began to rouse.

The woman's eyes were wild as she looked around her at the strange faces. Her animal-like growling evolved into an unintelligible babble and then more language like mutterings which drew on as the crowded market emptied and the sun began to set. Soon after the final patrons started to make their way toward home and the merchants began closing their shops.

A fierce roar issued from the woman and all heads turned to see the scarlet wife glowering over the bound woman, its dreadful clawed hands and open iron toothed maw going in for the kill.

The thing reached for the woman but Tishimi's Katana, imbued of the spirit of her father sang from its sheath. It was for a single stop motion moment as if the Al Karisi and the sword merged.

Radiance from the puncture and brilliant light as the crimson witch glowed as molten glass. As hot as the heart of a volcano. In the forge fire of the glowing, searing mass the blade of Tishimi's katana was ice blue death, caused the molten glass magma to seize.

All was as abrupt silence as it had been deafening noise less than a heartbeat earlier. The hag's outstretched hand slowed but reached just far enough to cause a fracture that spiderwebbed out from the place where the katana penetrated the torso of molten glass.

The fracture radiated out in frigid bifurcation as the blade super cooled the viscous semisolid magma-like body.

The red witch shuddered as it reached for the woman in defiance. With a thunderous crack it shattered into fine lime green glass powder.

Tishimi withdrew the blade and in one sharp motion flicked every fleck of glass residue from the blade and sheathed it.

A savage gale surged and took every trace of the glass powder away. Again, all was unnerving stillness. A moment passed, two and Ralf pointed skyward where the clouds over the moon parted.

"There hangs the lowest, brightest moon I have ever seen in all my years upon the sea." Sinbad gasped.

Tishimi, relaxed somewhat but still on her guard said, "Perhaps we could admire it at sea."

"I am ready to leave this place and be back aboard the Blue Nymph." Ralf concurred with Tishimi.

As they turned to go, mounted warriors, whom they had not seen approach, blocked their way. Sinbad started to go around the horsemen, but Tishimi struck a defensive posture and Ralf reached for his axe. Only then in the bright moonlight did he realize that they were surrounded by no less than a dozen black pajama clad warriors.

Sinbad drew his scimitar, "We have no quarrel here, with any in this place or with you. We are returning to our ship."

As he spoke, a white woman, not to say Caucasian, her skin was the color of bleached linen, her hair the color of the finest silver in the moonlight and her eyes as black as volcanic glass.

"We-we're, we are traders from Al Basra," Sinbad said slowly as the woman approached.

Her aspect grew with every step as she approached. As she stood before them, her physical body, head and shoulders taller than Ralf, her countenance impressed their submission. She spoke in a great and godlike voice that did not come from her mouth but was felt as much as it was heard, "You are known to us, blue eyed son of the Nubian Prince. Sinbad El Ari, pilot of the dhow christened the Blue Nymph. Your exploits are legendary even among the gods. This night you must travel to the place where the sisters weave the fabric of time and begin your quest to return Nergal to the hellish fires of the underworld. You must stop the god of war, pestilence and death from entering the temple at Yazili Kaya. He seeks his sword, to unseat the twelve and overthrow Teshub and lower a veil of eternal night. You must return his sword to the stone. He has struggled through all eternity to free it. He must not wield the sword."

Wide eyed, Sinbad lowered his scimitar, "How will I find this sword?"

A single rider rode up to Sinbad and dropped something at his feet.

Sinbad knelt and laid his scimitar in the dust. He took the oilcloth wrapped parcel, it was far heavier than he would have imagined, and unwrapped it. Within was a massive bronze and iron broadsword with a wide, thick blade, measuring seven hands.

"Beware Anatolia, death travels on the wind in the land of Corum. Time draws nigh Sinbad the sailor and you must not fail for consequences are dire. Go now to your ship and provision for your destiny. Direction will be provided, you must go to Hattusa of the Hittites, and you must find your way underground at Yazili Kaya there stands a temple of green glass, only there can

Nergal be sent back to hell. You must enter the temple and return the sword to the stone upon the altar. Do you accept your challenge?" Her otherworldly voice cut through to his very soul.

"Let us suppose I accept this challenge as you call it, and we succeed in returning this sword and Nergal to the underworld. What do we gain?" Sinbad asked.

"Your mortal world shall continue as you know it, pathetic as it is. If you do not take up this quest all you know shall be engulfed in Nergal's fire and your world will burn. You must decide Sinbad Al Ari. Do you commit your heart, your ship and all who serve you to the perils you must face to defeat the harbinger of death?" The ubiquitous voice grew in pitch, becoming more intense.

Sinbad knew that there was but one choice. It only appeared to be so. He doubted that they would be allowed to leave otherwise and though he had the utmost faith in Ralf and Tishimi, to waste their lives against a goddess and her Medjai was a fool's wager. Sinbad was no fool.

"I accept your challenge, but my friends must make their own decision. They are not my servants, though they travel in my company." He said, resolute.

"I Ishara hold the contract of your fate. Complete your quest and you and those in your service shall be released. Fail to do so and you shall be damned. Find your way with the Northman's compass, to the gates of Hattusa, go now Sinbad the sailor."

Her soulless obsidian stare burned into Sinbad's heart and his resolve was as unyielding as Damascus steel. "We must go."

The moment he spoke Ishara transfigured into a creature with the body of a scorpion with the torso of an armor-clad female warrior. She saluted with her sword and shield before galloping off into the night, her pajama clad warriors wafted away on the breeze.

Time passed. How long, it was unclear. When Sinbad arrived at his senses, he realized Ralf was kneeling a few paces away examining tracks in the packed earth of the market square. The night remained clear and there was no haze or still billowing dust from the departed horsemen.

Ralf took a handful of dust and rubbed it between his hands and smelt it for a long moment. He took another and held his clenched fist out and stood before letting the dust fall back to earth. Which it did at an unnaturally slow speed, almost sparkling in the brilliant light of the troubled moon. "They were here. Yet aside from these aged hoof marks, there is no trace. No dust. No sounds, no vibration, no smells. As if it were all,"

"A dream," Sinbad finished.

He drew the long dagger pointed iron and bronze sword from its oilcloth wrappings and held it high by the two-handed hilt. The moonlight shone on the wide, thick uniquely grooved blade leading down to the guard of eclipsing sun and moon. The shadow on the ground reminiscent of points on a map.

"There!" Ralf exclaimed, pointing out the route they must follow in the dirt. "Do not move. I must create a cartograph."

From a pouch hung on his great belt Ralf produced a roll of hide, a bone stylus and a flask of ink derived from wood ash and iron oxide boiled in oil. He laid out the hide so the shadow from the sword fell upon it and he smoothed it as best he could and weighted the corners with stones.

When the hide was situated to his satisfaction Ralf drew out as much of the detail as he could, then standing away to observe and returning to draw further features. His final notation was to add the waypoints indicated by the shadow of the sword's figured pommel.

"If all goes well, our destination is about four days walk from here." He gestured northeast, "We must first make our way from the lowlands and into the hill country." Ralf said, standing up and looking down at the map that he had drawn.

Sinbad lowered the sword and returned it to its wrappings. "Omar, take the boy and the materials to the Blue Nymph and return with provisions for a week. You will find us on the road north out of Mersin.

"Yes Sir, I will have Haroun get the new crew squared away and bring the hardiest of the lot with the supplies. Anything else?" The old Sindhe sailor asked as he shouldered his burden and steered the lad toward the docks.

"Make haste, for I foresee the events of this night as an omen of things to come. Beware trouble on the wind." Sinbad said as he shouldered the parcel containing the sword and adjusted its carry that it did not affect access to his scimitar.

Omar nodded over his shoulder and considered the troubled moon overhead as he bustled off with the boy in tow in the direction of the harbor.

"Let us depart now, the easterly leg of or travels should take us less than a day and we could strike northward twenty leagues by evening." Ralf urged and he rolled the map and stowed away his stylus and ink.

Omar and his small party of sailors did not depart the Blue Nymph until the noon hour. After giving Haroun instruction and getting the supplies stowed below decks it was after three in the morning and he'd needed food and sleep. Though his slumber was brief, a fleeting three hours, he arose with the cockerel's call at just before six and went up on deck as the boatswain signaled the change of watch.

"Master Omar, Sallah and Kenji have prepared provisions for twenty men for two weeks. I estimate this is twice the supplies needed for your journey plus something extra as Captain Sinbad insists on being prepared." Haroun called as he rode down a knotted line and raised his relief toward the crow's nest at the top of the mast.

"Thank you, Haroun. Are the men ready?" Omar asked, looking pleased despite his irascible demeanor.

"Master Haroun! An Akkadian merchant insists on speaking with Master Omar or Captain Sinbad." Elijah, a sturdy sailor in charge of security called from the head of the gangway.

Omar shot Haroun a look and motioned him to follow.

"I am Lokai, I bargained with your Captain Sinbad for a quantity of Pep'per of juniper." The slight fellow said without a smile, though his eyes lit in recognition at the sight of Omar.

Omar gave a slight nod at the man and turned to Haroun. "Have Korah prepare apple tea and kebabs for our guest.

The fellow raised his hand and shook his head. "Please pardon my rudeness. I appreciate your courtesy, but I must claim the juniper berries and hurry to join our caravan. We are leaving for Antalya."

"Do you have food and water for your journey?" Omar asked, slightly insistent as is the custom of the region.

"I do, and again thank you. I will have my purchase and take my leave." The fellow said with a bow.

Omar nodded to Haroun who called to two kibitzing sailors, "You there, Azar, Raza, go to the spice hold and bring our Akkadian friend the juniper berries that he purchased."

Omar turned back to Lokai, "My master said that you had agreed upon a stone weight, and you had paid him in rubies."

The man nodded, "Yes, fifteen."

"My master instructed me to tell you that he wishes to increase the quantity of berries because after your purchase the remaining quantity would make trading a chore because there are so few low volume buyers in the bazaars further east."

The Akkadian smiled, "Please thank your Master and tell him he is always welcome in the courts of my father, the Satrap Lokai.

"My captain will be pleased." Omar bowed.

Once the Akkadian's camel was loaded with a large sackcloth bundle of juniper berries strapped to either side, they said their goodbyes and he departed under an already hot late morning sun.

"Haroun, now that we have concluded the last of Captain Sinbad's trading,

I must leave you to continue our refitting efforts and getting the new crew situated. If you should need to find us, you will have to send a runner to Hattusa by the old north road toward Tarsus."

Haroun nodded and waved to his Master and friend as he and the five sailors went ashore and disappeared into the gathering throng of patrons moving alongshore toward the bazaar.

Ralf led Sinbad, Tishimi and Henri east along the coast road to the edge of Mersin proper and took the track northeast toward Tarsus. The heavily travelled road was dry and dusty but easy to navigate. Clouds traversing the sky beneath the bright moon showed foreboding signs of dangers yet to come, but not one of the party noticed. Not even Tishimi, who was usually in tune with such things.

As the Deli Cay River babbled in its bed, Sinbad stretched and skipped a flat stone across its surface. "Let's rest here for a while and we will continue."

Tishimi dropped her pack and knelt at the edge of the water to drink.

Ralf followed suit and drank deeply, before plunging his head beneath the water's surface and raising it skyward a moment later, brushing back his long blond hair. "Henri there are large fish, see if you can spear one or two. I will make a fire."

"As you wish, *mon frere.*" Henri stepped up onto a tree root and in one fluid motion nocked a special barbed arrow and drew his bowstring, rotating his gaze from Ralf to the surface of the water. A moment later, his eye and bow moving as one, Henri drew a breath and released the arrow on the respiratory pause.

Thrum-Splashwauck!

The arrow sank into the soft muck a couple of feet in front of Ralf. He shot Henri a look and reached for the arrow. He pulled it free of the mud and raised two thick, arm-length fish with it, writhing and wriggling as they broke the surface of the water.

"Ask, and you shall receive it." Sinbad laughed as the fish splashed Tishimi.

Ralf kindled a small fire and cleaned the fish. He pinned them to a sacrificial wooden plank and placed it over the fire. As the sap began to boil in the wood, he adjusted the plank. He braced up one edge and after a while tilted it in the opposite direction. When the scales began to rise, he removed the fish from the fire and sliced it lengthwise, making four long filets serving one to each of them. Once they'd eaten and to adoring compliments, Ralf consulted the map, and they continued north along the Deli Cay to the shallows above the deepwater gap.

Near Asaghi Burhan the party turned eastward toward Tarsus. Henri ranged ahead and Tishimi laid back as the rear guard. Periodically Ralf consulted the map and corrected the course as necessary.

In the late afternoon with the western sun beating at their backs Ralf led them around the southern edge of the small village Kerimler. There was very little evident traffic in the village proper, though the smells of meat cooking and sounds of music were evident in the distance.

As they stopped to rest under a Joshua tree Henri came in from the north and after a few minutes, Tishimi came in from the west.

"We need food. Henri did you see any merchants?" Sinbad asked.

Henri gave Sinbad a devious grin, "You are in luck my Capitan. I acquired enough brazed goat and labneh for a couple of meals. Sadly, they were out of capon and sherry, so this will have to do."

Henri opened his haversack and laid out a small parcel. They ate and resumed their journey.

At nightfall they paused to rest at the mouth of a cave. As they settled in for the night it began to rain, causing them to seek shelter in the cave. As they moved inside, the last thread of the failing daylight showed the corner of the small room and a pile of dry wood.

Observed by malevolent eyes from the shadows, Ralf fished in his pack for his flint and steel. Something watched from the comfortable, dangerous darkness as he located a bit of char cloth and struck a blaze.

As the tiny flame flickered and caught Ralf fed it dry litter and then laid on larger wood until a small but good fire lit and warmed the cave against the chill of the rain. Tired from the long days walk, the group's idle chatter soon died away to slumber.

Omar led the crew of new sailors out of the port of Mersin and Eastward along the coastline. His old bones did not appreciate the forced march, but he planned to catch up with Sinbad and the others before nightfall. Ralf's navigation skills were supreme and Omar already knew that the pace the man would set on a mission would make catching up a deliberate and concerted effort.

"Let's look lively lads, Captain Sinbad is waiting, and we cannot disappoint him." He said trying to motivate the young sailors and instill confidence in them and himself.

In the late afternoon they reached the Deli Cay River and crossed over it just north of where the narrow river emptied into the sea south of Karicailyas.

Once across the river they paused to take a brief rest. The faintest scent of rain was in the hot summer breeze.

Omar squeezed a few pints of wine from a full wineskin and passed it to the most junior man. "Take a little and pass it to the next man. We need to catch our breath and get back on the trail."

He was interrupted by the braying of an ass and the bleating and bah-bahing of sheep and goats.

The tinkling of shells tied to a shepherd's crook drew his attention before he saw an old man with a long beard come into view. Followed by a young man who carried a tiny kid in the crook of his arm, and a field dressed lion slung across his shoulders.

Omar went to greet the old man.

The old fellow smiled and said something in an unfamiliar tongue. He tapped his crook on the hard packed earth and the shells tinkled. The flock stopped and began to graze.

"Where is the old road to Tarsus?" Omar asked, looking from the old man to the boy and back again.

The pair looked back at him vacantly. Omar repeated the question but neither responded.

He looked around in irritation and one of the young sailors, the youngest came over and spoke with the old man in the local gibber.

The old man's smile was broken by missing teeth, but he pointed to the northeast and said, *"Al Basti! Eshab-i Kehf Magarisi! Al Basti!"*

The boy listened at length and then shook his head. He gestured vaguely northeast and said, "That way Master, but..."

Omar snarled and raised an eyebrow, "Well, out with it Boy!"

The old man and the boy were moving away with the flock and the young sailor watched them go.

"Well?" Omar growled.

"Nothing Master, we go that way." He pointed. "The rest is just a tale a mother tells. Demon riders with brass teeth and iron nails who make bad dreams for bad children."

They shared a measured look, but the young sailor maintained eye contact.

"Men, we are moving now." Omar ordered and marched off toward the northeast double time.

The men made haste but despite their pressing onward, their fleeting efforts were soon shrouded in darkness.

Omar led the men up a slight draw and crested a hill. As they rounded the top Omar came to a stop and tipped his nose to the wind, He smelled the distinct odor of wood-smoke and turned to walk directly toward it. The soft glow of a campfire came into view as the men gathered at the mouth of the cave.

" HENRI, DID YOU SEE ANY MERCHANTS. "

Omar raised a finger to his lips and signaled the men to follow him into the cave.

As they entered the room, it was immediately obvious something was off.

Sinbad cried out in his sleep as if he might wake.

Ralf thrashed about and cried out but also did not sleep.

Henri muttered something that sounded like a prayer in French.

Omar was drawing his dagger when Tishimi screamed, *"Warui yuma no akuma!"*

The Al Basti astride her chest flashed a demonic jagged brass toothed snarl. The demon hissed as Tishimi struggled awake.

As the samurai began to fight in earnest the demon glared and her and wailed, raising an iron clawed hand.

Omar kicked the demon square in the chest and launched himself on top of the evil thing, plunging his dagger where it would do the most good. The other sailors followed suit. Attacking the creatures, which were oddly unaware of their presence until their victims began to rouse.

Olan, the eldest of the new sailors approached the Al Basty that held Ralf's beard like a bridle.

"Get off and be gone!" He yelled, giving the creature a shove and stepping down on Ralf's hand. The Northman yowled in pain, suddenly awake.

The demon launched itself from Ralf's chest, going for Olan's throat. It latched on with its brass teeth and slashed wildly at the sides of the terrified man's neck.

Blood sprayed and ran in a thick, dark river that appeared black in the firelight.

The others killed the demon, but it was too late for Olan.

As all attention centered on their vain attempts to render aid to Olan. Sinabd still lay beneath the demon riding his dreams through the netherworld. As he cried out, his eyes rolled open and he was suddenly aware of the demon. They locked eyes and the demon wailed.

Sinbad thought first of the scimitar, unwieldy and out of reach on this occasion, he began to struggle when he felt a familiar presence at his waist when the demon again settled into its ride.

Tearing a hand free, Sinbad plunged a hand into his sash and pulled free the jewel encrusted dagger secreted there. Before the Al-Basty could react, Sinbad plunged the blade deep into the demon's liver.

Its gaping maw leered, it raised an iron clawed hand to counterattack and collapsed in a heap, its brass teeth mere hairs from Sinbad's jugular.

After the battle with the Al Basti there was little appetite for food or sleep.

"So much for a night's rest!" Henri complained.

"Better we move on from this place of death." Sinbad directed and shouldered his burden, followed by the others.

In the faint moonlight Sinbad and the others departed the cave of the sleepers to the northwest.

They followed a wide and well-worn path that narrowed as they traveled farther along. Going slowed as the terrain became rough and rocky as they journeyed north.

After a while the incline became steep. Sinbad slipped and slid back the six paces he had advanced.

"Ralf, what does your cartograph say about this?" Sinbad inquired as he got to his feet and pitched a stone at the unforgiving slope.

Ralf dropped his pack and the others followed suit, taking a few moments' rest as the Northman unrolled the hide on which he'd drawn the map.

"The map shows we are on course. My advice is to follow the terrain westward and search for a pass."

Sinbad followed Ralf's direction and oriented himself according to the map and observed the Viking's indications. He looked up the rise at the loose stone now more visible in the light of false dawn.

"I see little choice if we wish to arrive at Hattusa in one piece," Sinbad quipped.

Ralf stowed the map and pulled on his pack as he stepped around the rise looking for a pass north through the rugged country.

Hours passed as Ralf led the group over the rough terrain. Eventually the worn track became little more than a goat path. The trail ended at a sheer rock face into which a rough staircase had been hewn into the white stone.

Sinbad signaled everyone to drop their packs and went to the foot of the stairs.

"I'm afraid there's no way around. We either go back, or we ascend and face whatever lies beyond." Ralf advised.

"Thus, it is a metaphor for life," Sinbad mused.

He looked over his shoulder and called, "Henri, you and Tishimi ascend the staircase to reconnoiter and return to report what's up there."

"No problem, Mon Captain. It will be our pleasure." Henri rattled as he nocked an arrow. "I will signal when all is clear."

"Stick a sock in it, Froggy and don't get me killed." Tishimi drew her katana and held the sword down and to her rear as she huddled low and quickly began to ascend the stairs.

Henri followed, but his height and keen eyesight would be of little use in the confined space as they climbed at such a steep angle.

Tishimi's small silhouette was perfectly suited for moving in such confined quarters such as the narrow passage up the stairs through the rock face. She was very adept at using the shadows and the irregular surfaces of the hewn stone to conceal herself and move from concealment to concealment with relative speed.

Try as he might the usually stealthy Frenchman had a more difficult time providing overwatch for the lady samurai he followed.

The passage was a natural choke point and easily defensible from above. But all was quiet. Too quiet. It was setting Henri's nerves on edge.

He missed a step and his foot planted hard to steady himself. As his weight shifted, he extended his bow arm exhaled slowly as his weight settled. As he loosened his death grip on the bow the arrow slipped free and clattered loudly onto the stone steps, shattering the silence.

Henri gasped as the arrow bounced thrice and rolled toward the crevice at the right edge of the steps.

At the sound of the shaft on stone, Tishimi turned sharply and shot Henri a look, just as an arrow whistled past her.

Henri grabbed the arrow from the air as it flew, nocked it as he turned and aimed in the direction from which the arrow had come.

Nothing.

No sound.

No movement.

No archer at the top of the stairs.

Nothing.

Henri recovered his own arrow and quietly crept to a single pace behind Tishimi who was watching the pillared archway a mere dozen feet ahead.

When she heard Henri behind her, she covered the distance in a flash. Henri was right behind her. From behind the pillars they observed the ancient courtyard. It was empty except for a bubbling fountain.

"Who shot the arrow?" Henri whispered.

Tishimi moved from one shadow to the next and listened for a long moment.

When the sounds of insects and birds resumed, she looked up at Henri and nodded.

The Frenchman drew and released two arrows in a flight arc in the direction from which they'd come.

The four new crewmen, led by Omar were the first to emerge from the stairs and onto the limestone courtyard. Tishimi meditated near the bubbling fountain while Henri surveyed the valley below from the parapet.

Omar set his sailors to setting out a simple meal of kebaps and he walked the length and breadth of the small courtyard, impressed with the neatness of it.

Rafi appeared next, immediately followed by Ralf and Sinbad.

"Captain, I have the haji's preparing food before we embark." Omar addressed Sinbad.

"Finally, something to appease the ogre in my stomach." Ralf growled as he took out the map and prepared his compass and sunstone.

Rafi went to the fountain and lowered a hand into the bowl. He noticed how clear the water was. He cupped several handfuls and raised his ladled hands to just beneath his nose and inhaled.

The water smelled slightly sweet. He tasted just enough to wet his tongue, the sipped a bit more before drinking deeply. "If you thirst, this water is clear and sweet." Rafi declared.

Sinbad took a kebap from the open pouch laid out before the new sailors and went to the fountain.

He dipped a cupped hand and raised it to his lips. "Agreed, let us not leave this place without everyone filling their water skins."

Henri stepped down from the parapet and walked over to the seated party. He took a kebap and took one to Ralf, "I believe we can follow a river northward."

Ralf took the kebap and began to eat as he surveyed the expanse of valley and compared it to the crude map he'd drawn on the shore at Mersin.

Ralf found the relative time and oriented the sun compass to the correspondent hour. He stood before the map and compared it to the valley.

In the distance the sun glimmered on the surface of water, and he knew Henri was correct. Though small, the waterway snaked northward through the steppes toward the mountains across the valley and disappeared in the dark, dense forest that rose up to meet them.

"You have a good eye my friend," Ralf finished his kebap.

"I will scout ahead by a league to find out path," Henri said to the group as he refilled his water skin and pulled his pack onto his back.

The steppes from the limestone parapet and courtyard were a broad and naturally terraced prairie grassland. Several springs blessed it with lush green oases, which were set out in paddocks near ponds with a sparse farm or two with roaming shepherds and their flocks.

Henri moved through this pastoral land quickly and quietly. At varying intervals, he paused to watch the grass sway or observe the movements of the flocks of sheep and goats.

He lay for an hour on an outcrop to watch a passing caravan. The gypsies kept to themselves. Though their presence and movement were not wrong, the way their brigade moved and passed with strange purpose did not feel right to him. He watched them go and then crossed their track quickly.

By the heat of the day, Henri had crossed the greater breadth of the steppes and rested in the shade of a great stone. As tiredness crept through him and settled in his shoulders and legs, Henri's eyelids grew heavy. His usually active mind settled. His hearing remained alert.

It was during this time of rest that Henri realized that someone was following him.

The sound of the grass rustling in the breeze reverberated from the rock against which he rested. The gentle, even rustling noise,

Shuh, shuh, sh, shuh was suddenly interrupted. Shuh, shrup, shuh, shuh.

Henri realized that someone was not walking in the worn track but trying to move stealthily through the prairie grass.

Henri, stealthy as a cat, crawled to his feet and nocked an arrow as he moved. Creeping quietly, he rounded the stone and ascended the rear crags to the top where he low crawled forward to observe the prairie in hopes of catching sight of his pursuer.

In the distance across the sea of buffering prairie grassland he could see the party of sailors led by Ralf and Tishimi with Sinbad and Rafi at the center and followed by Omar and his new crew that had immediately been pressed into service.

Closer, Henri noticed a lambing ewe and a shepherd boy. The lamb bleated and he could hear her panting breath, faster momentarily and then two long bleats followed by one cut short followed by excited cries from both the boy and the ewe.

He saw nothing that concerned him, yet Henri could not shake the feeling that he was pursued.

The feeling stuck with him as he climbed down from the rock. He made his way further along and reached the edge of a stream that seemed to originate from a series of fantastical limestone and calcite formations which flowed from an outcropping of rock which contained the stream and did so until it disappeared into the tree line of a dark and dense forest.

Sinbad led the band of adventurers down from the parapet and across the prairie steppes toward the distant forest and the mountains that loomed beyond.

Ralf ranged fifty yards ahead of the group and Tishimi trailed as rear security. Omar and his sailors were a comfortable distance behind Sinbad, but the group traveled at a brisk pace under the afternoon sun.

Ralf thought of the rugged terrain and the paddock farms that dotted the inland landscape. His thoughts turned briefly to home and missed that life. He ranged east to west and back across the beaten track and searched the horizon for signs of trouble along the way.

In the distance a gypsy caravan crossed the prairie. Raffi pointed out the odd-looking wagon drawn by four asses.

"Your eyesight is good indeed for an old man." Sinbad joked with the sage physician.

"Not so keen as it once was. My sense of smell has not wanted with age and this prairie has the scent of a thousand herbs. Some strong, some gentle, done precious and others deadly to poison a hundred generations." He picked off several handfuls of leaves as they passed numerous and varied vegetation on their way.

"You'll not be offering me any of that tea!" Omar growled.

Raffi started to retort.

"Nor I," Sinbad concurred.

"Neither of you need this medicine. Maybe something to cool your libido, Omar." He scolded. Then to Sinbad, "Or your vanity."

Ahead, Ralf noticed a ruffle in the prairie grass as the breeze pushed it toward the distant forest and the mountains beyond. He watched the long grass buffet on the breeze and followed the wash of blowing blades as they bent toward the mountains.

Then the grass bowed in deference to some unseen object but beyond continued to wash on the wind past whatever it might be in pursuit of the distant forest.

On the horizon Ralf saw something or someone moving atop a distant boulder. As he moved forward, he continued to watch the grass rippling and again noted that it seemed to move around something, and that something was moving toward that boulder.

He glanced back at Sinbad and the others. They followed closer than one hundred yards and he knew without question they would follow his lead.

Ralf quickened his pace and as he reached the top of the next rise the sun reached its zenith. His view of the valley cleared, and two disturbing realizations settled on him.

The man on the boulder was Henri. The object in the field, the one indicated by the avoidant behavior of the buffeting grass, was mere feet from the base of the stone where Henri was reconnoitering the valley.

Ralf glanced again at the top of the boulder in the distance and Henri was gone. He scanned the horizon for the predator lying in wait and Henri the archer, or any sign of him.

Ralf glanced away from the glare of the sun. In the direction the gypsy caravan had gone. He returned his gaze to the shadow of the boulder and caught the merest glimpse of Henri's receding silhouette.

Ralf planted his feet and drew his bearded axe. He growled as he spun the axe over hand. He glared at the distant spot where the prairie grass still rippled around something.

Sinbad, alert to Ralf's pause, sprinted to his side. The others trailed a dozen paces behind as he reached the Northman's side. "What has drawn your attention, Son of Gunnar?"

Ralf indicated the boulder across the steppe. "Henri was there. Then he indicated the ocean of prairie grasses ebb and flow. "He was being stalked by something. The grass moves around it, there," he pointed to the place mere yards from the boulder. "Now both have moved into the forest beyond."

Sinbad stroked his beard, "Henri was scouting for a river."

"It is indeed there. I have seen the sun indicate the water. But Henri is being hunted." Ralf's knuckles were white as he gripped the axe handle.

"Henri is cunning, but your instinct is not remiss. Go to him and we shall follow closely." Sinbad nodded toward the forest and rested a hand on the hilt of his scimitar.

Ralf nodded and was off. He stepped off the beaten track, ranged a little to pick up the trail of whatever was stalking Henri.

He noticed a little crimped grass and circled it. He found a bit more and a few mashed seed heads. A pace further, he found the same but a few inches to the left and slightly ahead of a similar pattern. He glanced in the direction of the boulder and was off.

Sinbad watched the Norseman stalking his quarry and for a moment felt a tinge of remorse for whatever creature had made the misguided and malign decision to hunt Henri.

He turned to the remaining party and said, "We must redouble our pace. Ralf is ranging ahead to ensure Henri is safe. We must meet them at the river."

Ralf stormed through the forest in a headlong run. His bearded axe borne before him at the ready. Despite his size he ran at a considerable speed with impressive agility. He hurtled fallen trees and leapt from stone to stone at speed when necessary.

He followed the trail through the forest to a draw guarded by two massive Joshua trees. He leapt onto a stone and hurtled the knotted roots of one of the trees. The abrupt drop beyond caught him by surprise.

He landed in a crouch on the woven roots of another tree and without missing a step, ascended several uneven stones as if they were a staircase. At the top he jumped over a tangle of roots into open air.

Thinking quickly as his gut quaked and his body fell, Ralf hooked the beard of his axe blade over a rope like root.

Unrattled by the sharp jerk or rapid change of direction, Ralf plunged the long blade of the sea axe up to the hilt into the mudbank and exhaled as his weight settled.

After a momentary effort to pry loose the sea axe he climbed hand over hand, or knife over axe in this case to pull himself aloft to a place firm enough to regain his feet and continue.

As he stood, Ralf looked down into the ravine at the sun washed bones of more than one beast as a warning and epitaph to look before leaping.

He shook off the adrenal rush and returned to his pursuit when something rushed by so close that he parried by instinct and was left with the scent of sweaty wet hair and the rancid stench of unwashed flesh.

He shot a look left and right and saw nothing. He heard only the shuffling of forest creatures and the cacophony of their calling.

He ran twenty paces, stopped to listen and covered another fifty and darted behind a tree to listen again.

He turned to step off in the direction of the river when something spooked the forest birds and thousands exploded skyward from the trees.

Someone or something brushed him, moving fast and leaving him only with the stench of decay and deep iron claw marks in his wide heavy leather belt.

Ralf recoiled and sneered as he parried, his forearm catching only air and the faintest hint of the receding form.

He heard rustling in the grass and the woody rattle of dried browse. He turned again and this time the demirkiynak rushed him headlong trying to drive her iron nails into his belly, shrieking death.

Ralf brought down the butt of his axe handle on the top of her head and she fell in a heap at his feet.

He looked down at her and remembered something an ancient mariner had told him about a woman of the woods with iron claws and a thirst for blood. "This creature fears water."

Ralf did not tarry. He ran off headlong to find Henri and the river.

Henri emerged from the forest at the edge of a low basin where clear icy blue water poured over travertine cliffs to feed a magnificent translucent river that flowed inside fantastic calcite banks as if stalactites and stalagmites were growing above ground for the world to admire such majesty.

Henri was awestruck. As he stared at the mesmerizing beauty before him, he was unaware of the ragged, wild-haired, sack cloth clad forest dwellers emerging from the tree line behind him.

The Erboru closed in silently on the unsuspecting Frenchman.

A second group, led by a younger, more aggressive male named Acura pounced, leaping toward Henri's exposed back, claws out, gaping maw open, poised to tear flesh.

The beast was torn from the air by Ralf Gunnarson who charged headlong from the woods to protect his friend.

Henri felt the sudden rush of air and rolled to his right, raising and drawing his bow as he skidded to a stop.

The archer's aim found its mark and he released the arrow.

The pack of Erboru converging on Acura where he wrestled for his life with Ralf scattered when Henri's bowstring thrummed.

An old Erboru, white bearded and long in the tooth batted the arrow aside and strode to where the pair grappled. He seized Acura and threw him off Ralf with apparent ease.

As the younger werewolf-like creature gained his feet, the pair exchanged some communicative growls and baring of fangs in a proof of dominance display.

The old Erboru didn't skip a beat or stop to check himself when Acura tried asserted himself. He stepped over the recovering Ralf and glowered over the smaller Acura.

Acura started a display but the elder slashed across his face with a clawed hand.

The welp winced and a yelp of pain escaped him, the elder slammed a fist into his jaw and rammed a knee where it would do the most good.

Acura collapsed and the older wolf man dragged Ralf to his feet.

The Northman had no sooner settled on his footing when he felt Henri beside him. "I do not believe they mean us any harm despite…"

"Despite?" Ralf spat.

Henri let the tension off his bowstring. "Because they followed me through the forest and only the young male challenged the elder's authority."

"There is a boat tied just there, behind you." Ralf growled.

"What about the others?" Henri queried.

"They're arriving presently." Ralf grunted as four young sailors burst forth from the forest driven by the wrath of their master Omar, whose constant stream of beratement and profanity still hangs over that part of Asia as a cloud of warning.

Tishimi and Sinbad emerged from the flanks along the riverbank to take up their blades in defense of their comrades.

"I see this party has drawn the most exotic guests," Sinbad observed.

"What did you do with Raffi?" Henri asked of Tishimi.

"He was just behind..." She looked over her shoulder and recovered her stance, sheathing her sword.

Acura lunged, slashing the old Erboru's throat. Blood sprayed and the old warrior's life ran down his chest in a river.

A roar of defiance passed Acura's fangs as the other Erboru massed to attack.

"I'm down here in the boat!" Rafi exclaimed.

Sinbad heaved the wrapped sword in Rafi's direction while drawing the scimitar from its sheath across his back. "Rafi guard this with your life. As you know it is the whole point of our quest."

The bundled sword struck Rafi across the chest, and he grabbed it, struggling to arrest its weight in an awkward basket catch.

Ralf cleaved bone and separated life from limb as Erboru came after him two and three at a time.

Tishimi took the fight to the wolfmen who threatened Omar and his sailors.

Sinbad defended Henri as he picked off Acura's lieutenants and tried to target their leader. As one of the Erboru attacking Omar fell, the old sailor shoved Eli toward the boat, "Prepare the vessel for our departure. We have to get out of here."

Eli sprang into action as soon as Omar spoke. He did not wait to be instructed but intuited what his master had thought to tell him. He slid down the bank, between two attackers and slipped loose the moorings before leaping aboard and calling out, "Master Omar, Ready Ho!"

Hearing the young sailor call out, one by one the adventurers found egress to the boat. Ralf gave it a final shove into the current as he sprung himself over the rail.

Henri shot several arrows toward the bank as the current caught the craft and it slipped away from the shoreline.

Acura raced down the bank to the water's edge and two Erboru ran into the water up to their waists when something ambushed Acura in a spray of blood and a scream of holy terror escaped him as the boat floated out of sight.

The river flowed to the north through the forest and toward the mountains. An hour further along the channel narrowed and the current picked up.

Henri stood in the bow of the craft and was abruptly aware of the sound of rushing water.

"Captain I am not sure, but I hear the sound of water rushing. That is unusually bad news."

Tishimi stepped over Ralf, who slept in the bottom of the boat with his feet propped on the skeg. She joined Henri in the prow and listened. "The sound is deeper, like water filling a jar."

Sinbad stepped cat-like onto the rail and stepped over Ralf, who snored and when he joined the pair in the front of the boat, he listened intently.

At first, he heard birds, a variety of insects and finally as he strained to hear, the slightest hint of rushing waters could be heard over the din.

"I barely hear it. You have fine hearing indeed. We must proceed with caution."

Omar watched the gathering at the bow from the stern, and when Sinbad nodded his agreement to Henri, he handed off the tiller to Eli, who grasped it and stepped against the shaft with a hip to maintain the course that the boat was on.

Omar stepped onto a pile of coiled line and onto the sleeping Northman's chest.

Ralf's eyes rolled open and as he stirred to turn over, Omar lost his balance and began to fall.

"Whoa!" Omar exclaimed, followed by a number of sworn oaths.

Realizing what was happening, the Viking seized Omar's planted foot with a huge hand and grasped his belt in the other, arresting his momentum and using Omar's weight to counterbalance and set him down with a little more grace than the first mate's dignity would allow.

"All right there Ralf, that's quite enough. I am capable of…"

Ralf released his purchase on the old sailor and the unsteady fellow fell into Sinbad who almost pitched over the rail.

"Nice of you to join us, my graceful friend," Sinbad chided.

"Master is all well?" Omar asked with an embarrassed grin.

"...HE JUMPED OVER A TANGLE OF ROOTS..."

"We must be wary. There may be rushing waters ahead."

The tiny flat bottom craft carrying her vagabond crew ran askew and began to spin on the rushing current.

Eli fought the tiller to correct the course, but the current was winning. "Master!"

Omar stepped into Ralf's chest again but leapt over the coil of line en route to assist his young protege.

Plying their combined weight and strength, they barely were able to budge the stubborn tiller. The long tiller bowed under the strain of their weight, and they were leery of snapping it.

Ralf rolled upright and came to assist as the boat swayed and turned on the current in a slow counterclockwise spin.

The Northman seized the tiller and piled steady pressure against the draft. After a moment both he and Omar shook their heads.

"No use in fighting it," Omar stated.

"No," Ralf concurred.

"Maybe we can make it right itself," Eli offered.

The two experienced seamen looked at him and started to shake their heads when Eli again spoke up.

"Steer into the spin and at the end in the river where the current changes, steer away and it will straighten," he directed.

"Lad, that will never work," Omar smiled and gave a very smug chuckle.

Ralf was more thoughtful and said, "Omar, it just may." He nodded to Eli, and they pushed the tiller hard a'starboard.

The shallow draft of the skiff needed no encouragement to follow the path of little resistance and it spun end around several times.

Eli held the tiller while Ralf looked ahead for the change in the river's course.

In the distance he could see they were approaching a sharp Eastward bend and said to Eli and Omar, "on my mark we must draw the tiller a'port and hold it there until the course is corrected.

Both men, young and old nodded their agreement and waited tense moments as the out-of-control craft spun on axis. Ralf watched for just the right moment.

"Now!" Ralf roared as the boat slipped past the point and around the bend.

The three of them gave the strained tiller a mighty shove hard to port as the skiff came around and the current shifted.

The prow swung about, and the men dug deep to give the tiller a final shove. As the craft listed and began to overcorrect, Ralf brought the tiller to center, and the boat nosed into the speedy current and raced toward the mountains and the ever-growing din of rushing waters.

Ralf released the tiller to Eli, who under the close scrutiny of Omar, guided the boat along its speedy tack, toward whatever lay ahead.

"Look there, Master!" Eli gestured to an opening in the mountain.

Omar turned his head and was astonished at the aspect of a sleepy old man's yawning mouth in the craggy bush covered mountainside.

Omar gasped, "The river...our boat. We shall be swallowed by it."

He had no sooner spoken and turned to alert the captain when Sinbad himself raised the alarm. "Be on your guard, my friends. Our journey is about to take another strange turn."

"Lamps! We need lamps!" Henri called and began to rummage in his haversack.

The others followed suit.

One by one they turned up nothing until Eli handed off the tiller to Omar and ducked into the tiny cabin. He emerged with several short staves of wood and a roll of oilcloth.

"Torches. We can make torches. If we can find any oil at all the cloth will last much longer."

"That's it, torches. Omar this young sailor is a credit to you!" Sinbad exclaimed as he held up a fold of the oilcloth for Henri to cut into strips.

Raffi lowered his head and scurried into the cabin. In the low light he searched the shelves for a bottle or flasks that had not been broken on the tumultuous trip down river, he found none. He opened a small chest and set aside several small soft bundles. In the bottom of the chest, he found several smaller boxes with fitted lids which he checked and set aside.

The final box rattled as he lifted it from the chest. He opened the hinged lid and inside he found a dozen partially filled bottles of varied viscosity.

He pulled one vial after another, holding it up just high enough to judge the color and set aside the four most amber of the oils. On deck, he sparingly dropped a bit of the amber liquid onto the oilcloth wrapping on the several stages of wood.

Ralf used flint and steel to light a spark on a large fragment of char cloth he pressed into a bird's nest of moss and punky wood he'd carried in his fire making kit.

One by one the torches were out and as the late evening's fading light turned to night the little boat passed through the cavernous mouth of the old man of the mountains and true darkness was upon her crew.

As the vigilant adventurers stood watch by torchlight in the absolute darkness of the cavern the river washed out into a glass calm subterranean sea.

As the boat slowed it was yet drawn farther into the cavern toward some as yet unknown and unseen destination the crew held stalwart and on guard each of them contemplating his own preparation for the personal and unknowable terrors that might lie ahead.

"Hold her steady, Eli." Omar directed his prodigious young sailor.

Eli, unseen but attentive stated, "Yes master."

The cool unmoving air was very damp and occasionally drops of condensation peppered the adventurers and caused their torches to hiss and sputter.

For an undeterminable amount of time, at least two full sleeps and the preparation and consumption of four meals, with changes of watch as the torches burned down, as determined by Ralf and Omar, who were instinctive seamen, who both concurred that with neither sun nor star to gauge time, they were counting based on the hours it took for the oilcloth binding on the torches to be consumed by the flames and burn away.

On the change of watch Ralf woke Sinbad, "Captain it is time for your watch."

Sinbad stretched and stood up, feeling the chill of the cavern, he rifled blindly through his haversack for a cloak, and moved Ralf's torch lower to provide more light for his searching. A moment later he pulled the woolen cloak from the sack and stood up. He pulled on the cloak and followed Ralf to the bow rail.

"Omar?" Sinbad asked.

"He has awakened Eli, his watch just ended." Ralf informed him.

"I need an account of our supplies and rations." Sinbad said quietly.

Ralf turned to the young sailor standing near the rail. "Bring your master to see the captain."

"Yes sir." The sailor held his torch before him and scurried arrear.

Several moments later the sounds of a scuffle, followed by the swearing of oaths in a variety of languages announced the approach of Omar.

"The sound of your approach announces your grace." The mirth heard, but the smile unseen in the darkness.

"Azar says you need to see me, Captain?" Omar growled, unamused.

"I need and account of our supplies and rations. We have been afloat now onto the third day on this underground sea, and nearly a week since leaving the Blue Nymph. Our provisions cannot last forever."

"Captain, I know that we only have two days prepared rations remaining for our entire party. There is a further two-day supply of Captain's rations and I have the dried grains as a last resort," Omar recited.

"Omar, I want you to divide my personal rations in with the rest, now is not the time for such luxury," Sinbad ordered.

"But Master, already the difference is sparing as it always has been on our adventures." Omar sounded pleading.

Times passing measured only by the flickering flames of burning oil cloth passed at an unnerving pace. Sparsely rationed food ran low and two full sleep cycles passed despite the watch schedule and the final changes of oil cloth were put upon the staves.

"This will be our final lighted watch," Sinbad said to Omar as he retired from his shift at the tiller.

"Master, we have but one last meal for the entire crew. We set lines but not a single fish has taken a hook with no bait to entice it." Omar conveyed news of which Sinbad was already aware.

"I am certain some turn of good fortune will see us through, but what that may be, I am as yet uncertain. Try to rest my old friend. We shall see what tomorrow brings." Sinbad bade him good night and then prayed as he stood the longest watch of his long time at sea.

The seemingly endless night dragged on. The oilcloth's final ember burned down and faded into darkness with an unseen curl of smoke. One by one, each torch burned its last. Hours passed in darkness and the only sound was an occasional cough or snore as each man slept.

In the cool damp of the true night the crew of the tiny vessel slept. A single torch's tiny flame was all that remained of the oilcloth and the tiny remnant of the oil. From time to time the condensation drizzled and somewhere a blind cave dwelling fish broke water.

Droplets of water pattered Tishimi's face, and she woke with a start. She sat upright and moved to her feet just as the boat ran aground and came to an abrupt and jarring halt.

Everyone was awake and there was chaos in the disorienting darkness.

One of the young sailors cried out as another stepped on him. Others scuffled, fearing they were under attack.

Lithe and fleet of foot, Henri leapt to the roof of the boat's small cabin.

Ralf separated the scuffling sailors, planting each against the knee high gunwhale.

Tishimi felt rough hands on her, and she slapped them away, each blow with greater force as she repelled the unseen threat. Her final strike was a short, sharp punch to Omar's nose.

"Ouch! Allah's beard, why did you hit me?" The old sailor cried.

"What were you searching for in my kimono?" She hissed.

"It's dark, I was not…"

"Silence!" Sinbad commanded and the crew ceased and desisted. The darkness was once again still.

"Omar, you and Eli sound the ship. Ralf, Henri, find where we are aground and if we have found land. Tishimi supervise the sailors, gather all supplies and make ready to go ashore."

Moments passed as the crew mustered to quiet purpose. Though the chaos of surprise had subsided, and the scuffle of disorientation persisted in the darkness.

Sinbad stood near the cabin door and heard in the distance the sound of feet wading ankle deep water and then walking in dry pebbles. The sound receded away despite the echo in the cavern.

"Master?" Omar's voice came to him from the darkness followed by the sound of the first mate tripping over something and a cloud of multi language profanity. "Who left this line here?"

A moment later Omar grabbed at Sinbad's arm, "Master?"

"Yes, Your Gracefulness?" Sinbad chuckled.

"Our boat may yet be seaworthy, but I fear not for long. She's taking on water through the cabin floor, and we have no tools to make the repair."

After a while the sound of feet tramping in dry gravel returned followed by trudging in damp pebbles and then ankle-deep water. A moment later Ralf was at the rail.

"Captain Sinbad, we have reached a shoreline. Perhaps this is the fabled underground city."

Sinbad had also heard the folk tales of an underground city. "So long as we can lay this sword to rest on the way to fill our sacks with treasure."

Each man was lashed together via the length of line from the boat lest they become lost in the dark. After a while the dry pebbled shoreline gave way to sand, loose dirt and finally packed earth.

"Captain, ahead I see a point of light. It is faint. Shall I go reconnoiter?" Henri asked.

"You have keen sight. You and Tishimi go and report what you find." Sinbad instructed.

Henri and Tishimi bounded off into the night, their receding footfalls separated into long running strides. After a few moments the sound subsided to quiet and then silence.

"Let's wait quietly while our scouts are ranging ahead." Sinbad said, trying to soothe the nerves of the road weary adventurers, as well as his own.

Henri and Tishimi hurried quietly away from where the party waited. At first Henri moved directly toward the faint green point of light until the grade of the cavern floor changed.

As the land rose, he took a wide arc around the rise but moved generally back toward the light.

Henri circled around the rise and the faint light dimmed out of sight he continued his track, mentally calculating distance and following until they came to an unseen but felt stone retaining wall. He waited a long moment until he heard and then felt Tishimi beside him in the dark.

"How did you and Ralf ever find this in the dark?" Tishimi demanded.

"I do not know. I feel drawn here. Ralf bade me not to come, but I could not stop myself." the archer explained. "I just feel that I know where we are supposed to go." He stated it, though it sounded more like a question.

"Let's find that green light then and return that sword to its resting place." Tishimi said.

They followed the wall for one hundred paces and then one hundred more. Tishimi followed Henri and then he followed her, moving from pillar to pillar with twenty-five paces between.

Set out from one pillar a set of stairs carved into the stone rose into the darkness.

"Let's follow these stairs," Henry said to Tishimi, whom he thought was behind him.

"There appears to be that green light from up there somewhere." Her voice came from in front of him and slightly above. At the top of the stairs the parapet opened onto a small pavilion.

What appeared from a distance to be a green point of diffuse light was a beam of sunlight from an opening in the top of the cave reflecting off the dark algae water of a small pool with a long still fountain.

For long moments Henri and Tishimi observed the silent pavilion. No man moved. No creature stirred. It appeared that they were alone in the green tinted semi darkness.

Eventually they began to let their guard down. Tishimi rose from the landing followed by Henri. Quiet and cat-like they moved around the top of the parapet skirting the pavilion and meeting at the rear where more steps led upward, and another stair led down into darkness.

They did not explore the myriad openings, doorways, passages or further spaces. They met near the staircases and peered around again.

Finally, Henri said, "There are pyres along the parapet."

"We must find a way to light them and return to the captain." Tishimi replied.

"That would be no problem. I have a flint and steel, if the wood is dry then we shall have fire."

They moved quickly to the nearest pyre and found the wood to be slightly damp. However, a pile of browse and kindling nearby was quite dry as was a bundle of moss and grasses beside it.

Henri fished his fire-making tools from a pouch and handed them over to Tishimi. Minutes later a small fire was kindled which they fed and prepared both a portable fire and a torch so that they could reliably light their way.

The signal pyre burned bright behind them, and the others lit with little encouragement. They lit seven pyres in all as they made their way toward the steps down from the parapet from which they'd come.

"Return to the Captain and bring the rest of us safely here. I will set the remaining pyres alight and try to find out where we are and if we are any closer to the end of our journey." Henri directed and Tishimi started down the stone steps.

He watched for a long moment as the flame of her torch departed into the dark and her only reply was the stealthy footfalls leading away.

Henri took the portable fire to the next pyre and set it ablaze and continued around, lighting the fires until he came again to the two staircases. He fashioned another torch and began to search in earnest.

Just off the pavilion was an antechamber that Henri immediately recognized as a European style guardhouse. A small desk and several tiered bunks lined adjacent walls. A table and low stools were against the rear wall.

Henri returned to the pavilion and moved to the next doorway. This one was inset and behind a heavy barred door he found a stockade of sorts with four small austere cells with bronze caged doors.

The last salvageable items were handed over the rail to the two sailors whose names Sinbad had yet to learn. He marveled at how in the intense and oppressive absolute darkness how the usually irascible Omar had been as patient as a nursemaid with the youths who were little more than boys playing at being seamen.

"Are all ashore?" Sinbad called out.

"Aye, Captain! All present ashore." Omar called back.

Sinbad stepped over the rail and shouldered the bundled sword and his haversack. He walked ashore, feeling his way and taking care not to stumble.

"Captain, look there." Ralf called from nearby and Sinbad reflexively looked toward and then past the sound of his voice to a point in the darkness where the dim green point of light had bloomed into one and then another bright and beautiful yellow flames. Moments passed as more flames were lit and finally a single torch descended and fluttered into and out of view as it crossed the void of night.

Eli stood near Omar as Tishimi approached. The other young sailors kibitzed and complained about one thing or another. He listened to their gripes about having to carry bundled torch staves or the now coiled line, or a haversack of other supplies. As meager as those remaining provisions were; the fact that none of the lot of them were pulling their weight annoyed him.

As the circle of Torchlight announced Tishimi's arrival he reached for the coiled line and hoisted it up and over his shoulder. He settled the line in place and said, "Master, are we going to make use of the torches?"

"For the moment I think not." Omar said, but as Tishimi passed, he motioned for Eli to follow.

Tishimi went to Sinbad and reported. "Captain, Henri stayed behind to light the remaining pyres and begin exploring."

"We are ready, Tishimi. Lead us there," Sinbad ordered.

Omar spoke up. "Master, Eli has asked if we need the torch staves, we took from the boat?"

"We have no wrappings or oil, but it seems foolish to leave them behind." Sinbad lifted the bundled sword into the crook of his arm and then he smelled the oilcloth it was wrapped in. He glanced down at it.

Frustration welled in him as he realized that he'd had enough oilcloth to meet the need in his possession all along. "Omar, have one of your men bring those torch staves. Have Eli prepare them." Sinbad directed.

Omar turned to Eli who was loaded down with everything the others had disdained and lost his temper, "Azar, take that coiled line. Raza, take that tiny haversack of provisions. Eli, prepare the torch staves. The three of you must model the example of Eli, he seems to learn and to lead. The life of a sailor isn't a lark and your lot in life is about to get much more difficult.

Eli shifted his burdens to the other Sailors and took the bundled torch staves to where Sinbad waited next to Tishimi. He realized that this chore of preparing torches had been given to him an illustration to the others. Any of them could have done it, but they'd left their share to others. He was determined never to be one of them.

As the torches were lit and the expedition was underway Eli walked ahead of the group, just behind Tishimi, following her lead and trying to learn from her.

Omar was very pleased.

Sinbad carried the long heavy bronze sword at his side. It was truly a weapon meant for a larger heavier man than he. When Ralf held it, its heft had seemed toy like.

Sinbad thought about this mission to return the sword and wondered at the relative quiet of this part of the journey to do so during what he thought was the final leg of their adventure. His adventure. None of them would be here if not for him.

He heard them each in their way as they half marched in a torchlit column toward yet another unknown situation.

Although it was going well, too well, he felt the growing urge to hurry, he also desired for this adventure to come to a close. Sinbad shrugged off this feeling and increased his pace to walk abreast of the young sailor Eli and Tishimi who was leading them toward their destination and whatever fate Allah had in store.

When Tishimi reached the walls of the parapet she paused for the rest of the group to catch up.

She explained to Sinbad, "Two hundred paces and we will come to a stair that leads up to a pavilion." She gestured with her torch.

As the last of the group reached the wall, Tishimi proceeded to the stairs. They covered the distance quickly and anticipation filled each of them.

At the base of the steps the group gathered. Sinbad was about to speak when both Ralf and Tishimi bolted in a headlong race to the top. The sailors followed suit, moving with more purpose than Omar had seen from them since they'd set footboard the Blue Nymph.

Sinbad's foot had no sooner fallen upon the first stair when the thunder of hooves rumbled and the ground shook. He couldn't see the mounted troops, but he could hear and feel their coming. He ran up the stairs and yelled, "To arms!"

Dust was thick in the air and hoofbeats shook the ground as the unseen horsemen approached.

Tishimi stood her ground in front of the young sailors. Drawing her katana, she said a prayer to the ever-present specter of her father.

From some as yet unnoticed catacomb Henri ran headlong into their midst pursued by a phalanx legion of khopesh wielding skeletonized hoplite infantry. Their bronze shields, helmets and armor rattling against their decrepit bones. Fleshless mouths hissing some guttural unformed Hittite tongue, only one word discernible, "Nergal!"

Henri leapt upon the fountain and felled three of the soldiers with heavy arrows from the war bow he carried. Even as they fell, others stepped forward in their rank to replace them.

Ralf drew the bearded axe from his belt and stabbed another of the soldiers with the sea axe he carried.

The tongueless troops hissed and clicked in their unknown tongue only the emphasized name of Nergal discernible as their unified and emotionless attack continued.

Sinbad rushed into them, raising the broadsword and cleaving a broad swath only to have their scattered, rattling bones and clattering arms replaced by more of them, the phalanx closing, and another arriving to join the fight from the bowels of the cavern.

As he fought his way toward the fountain he yelled, "Henri?"

Henri shot a well-placed arrow that skewered one of the legionnaires through its mouth and the one behind it through an eye socket, both falling in a heap of inanimate bones and armor that clattered to the floor.

The archer nocked another arrow and drew the bowstring taut. He stepped off the fountain and onto the helmeted head of one of the attacking skeleton soldiers. Sidestepping a khopesh blade via another helmet, he released the arrow which drove home into the crevice between stones above the doorway from which the skeletal legion still poured. "There Captain, the catacomb leads to the mortuary temple of their sword god." Henri yelled above the melee.

Sinbad heard the sound of Henri's call, but the words were lost to the sounds of battle. He saw the arrow above the crypt entrance and surged to where Ralf was holding off the soldiers to protect Raffi, Omar and two of the sailors.

Tishimi's katana was a deadly blur. She was gradually advancing her attack and moving forward. Eli was at her side, wielding a dropped khopesh for all he was worth and holding his own. They were taking the fight from the fountain toward the catacombs.

Sinbad, stood shoulder to shoulder with Ralf, cutting down the skeleton army as they poured forth, three or four abreast. Yet more of them skittered and scurried along the walls and two columns clawed their way along the roof.

"Captain, there are too many." Someone's pleading voice was heard, but whose was lost in the din of hoofbeats.

Sinbad's reply was drowned out in the neighing, whinnying and staccato

"CAPTAIN, I SEE A POINT OF LIGHT..."

report of hoof on the white stone of the pavilion.

One, another and then all of the skeleton troops took notice of the approaching spectral horsemen and roared in unison, a terrible battle cry.

Sinbad reversed his grip on the sword to make a low block and the beam of sunlight from the roof passed through the sun and moon figured into the guard and time stood still.

The horsemen dressed in the garbs of the Medji swept across the pavilion from end to end. The spectral calvary rode down the guardian minions of Yazilikaya. Their swords separating spirit from bone.

Sinbad and the others, in the mystic perception of slowed motion began to press their advantage. In the confines of the crypt as they fought farther into the depths until at last the final skeleton fell under Ralf's axe and time again began to pass.

They made their way into an open gallery of sorts, the mortuary temple's hall of the gods.

One by one they entered, Ralf, Tishimi, Omar, followed by the pair of young sailors, Raffi, Henri and finally their leader.

When Sinbad entered with the sword, a brisk otherworldly wind started to blow.

Dust began to gather and integrate into muscle and bone. More than men, the Hittite gods formed, just as their aspects upon the walls, but meat and mettle, armed with sword and shield.

The storm god Nerik formed first, and the strong winds intensified. The other children of Kumarbi followed, one dozen in all, the warrior gods of Hittite myth and legend becoming flesh and bone before the adventurer's eyes.

All but One, Nergal, the god of death, owner of the sword Sinbad carried.

Ralf plunged his sea axe into the breast of a near figure, a god of the hunt with the head of a lion, but the blade merely passed through. Likewise the blade of his axe failed to find solid, earthly flesh or to cleave bone. Sand merely scattered, blown on the storm god's breath to integrate again.

Wurumkatte, the god of war standing at the front of the formation, though not quite fully formed, began to stir. First a finger, a twitch of the lower jaw, a foot strained to move, a hip to flex. The right arm and hand fought to move, tensing under restrained potential energy.

A column of skeletal soldiers flooded into the room retreating from the horsemen outside. Their clockwork mechanical motion attempting to form a phalanx and attack.

Henri shot arrow upon arrow until a dozen of them lay in the doorway. In disbelief he glanced away, but one last troop rushed straight for Tishimi's weak side, thrusting its bronze javelin.

Eli raised the khopesh he carried and leapt to intercept the spear.

Ralf cut down the skeletal warrior, but a moment too late. The javelin had already run Eli through, piercing a further ten inches from the back of the brave youth.

Omar's knife was out, a mere extension of his arm. The long, upswept curve of the wide blade sliced upward through the folds of fine linen robes of the guardian god to the left of Wurumkatte, his bow falling away unused.

At that moment the war god drew the long bronze khopesh sheathed at his side, bringing it up in a long, broad driving slash.

Sinbad blocked the strike, stepping in with the broadsword and saving Omar from being cleaved hip to shoulder.

The other gods engaged but were well matched. Henri's arrows found their mark, but against gods, they were largely ineffective.

Ralf, attacked by a pair whose twin aspects were oddly similar but oppisite. He managed to use their disadvantage of size skewering one and embedding his axe in the helmet of the other before slamming the pair together, disarticulating them.

Wurumkatte fought with neither inhibition nor fear. The ancient sword and extension of his arm, he wielded it relentlessly, looking for a weakness in Sinbad.

Omar knelt over the corpse of Eli, tears of rage running from his eyes. His knife was ready, but no attack came.

Nearby the two remaining sailors held off the few remaining skeleton soldiers whose power was waning.

After Eli had taken the spear meant for Tishimi, she leapt into the fight with an intensity that overwhelmed the mysticism that reanimated these long dead Hittite deities.

Wurumkatte was inch by inch gaining advantage over Sinbad and the draw was becoming a victory in the making.

Ralf came to Tishimi's side. "We must attack to free the captain, so that he may return the sword."

She nodded and drove the blade of her katana through the specter in front of her.

The adventurers massed and attacked the war god as one.

"Sinbad, the mortuary temple!" Henri yelled, shooting three arrows to cover the attack.

Sinbad rushed through the doorway to the resting place of Nergal. Inside the crypt, the empty hands of the sarcophagus lay waiting.

Sinbad took the sword by the hilt and blade and laid it in place. The gilded hands closed about it and lowered it against the statue's breast.

The moment the sword was set in place the savage wind reversed itself and in the vacuum of the true night it was all carried away, as in that bazaar where their adventure had begun.

Once by one, they came to in the shadow of the lion's gate at Hattusa, capitol city of the Hittites. They were standing in a circle and facing a line of mounted Medji.

"Sinbad, our people are forever in your debt. Please accept these tokens of our esteem, no matter how small and insignificant they may appear to the wider world, to us they are the world."

And they vanished in the breeze, leaving only a small wooden chest which contained a flask of oil and a small quantity of gold, myrrh and frankincense.

That small chest sat upon a larger chest filled with blue gold coins. A bundle of provisions lay nearby.

"No one shall ever believe this." Sinbad sighed.

Dawn was breaking overhead, and a rare desert rain began to patter on their heads bringing the group wearily to their senses. They gathered their belongings and the spoils of their adventure and began the trek back to the Blue Nymph.

Omar wept as he trudged along. Sinbad noticed and put a hand on his old friend's shoulder. "What troubles you, my brother?"

"We have sailed with many a young sailor, and we were all green seamen at one time. But Eli had a gift and a spirit of a true seaman. I will miss him."

Sinbad stopped and pulled a wineskin from the bundle of provisions and untied the flap. He raised it heavenward. "To Eli, may your soul rest in peace, and may your memory live on!" He drank deeply and passed the wineskin to every remaining member of the party.

## The End

# Essay

Last June, that is June of 2024 I had some white space in my calendar. I had just published the fourth book in my Champion City Series and was thinking about what came next, It was time for a break from my big city detective and the depravity he faces and time for a little writerly escapism. So I wrote Ron Fortier and asked for the specs on titles he was trying most urgently to fill. Sinbad was the first one attached to that email, so I dove in, watching the Ray Harryhausen Sinbad movies and rereading the Thousand Nights tales to try to immerse myself in the lands and culture that Sinbad calls home. I loved it as much this go around as I had when I first read and saw those films.

I knew almost immediately that I wanted to set my story in ancient Anatolia in Turkey. The area north of the Tarsus of biblical fame, in the lands of Asia minor once ruled by the Hittites, using Turkish, Hittite and Hurrian mythology and folklore to send Sinbad et al on what I hope is a tale of high adventure in a place that for me holds a captivating interest.

Having spent some time in Southwest Asia and visiting many of the places mentioned herein, I love the certain what if romance that these historic sites hold for those who care to learn history.

Many of these myths and legends are from separate eras on the historic timeline, but stitched together make for some fantastic fiction. I hope you enjoy reading this as much as I enjoyed writing.

J. WALT LAYNE - is an author, freelance writer and former columnist for The Albany Journal. He got his start writing articles for Ritchie's The Backwoodsman Magazine. His fiction credits include stories in a dozen new pulp and noir anthologies reviving characters from pulp's golden age. He is the author of the Champion City Series starring Thurman Dicke and Frank Testimony, a legal thriller. He is a veteran of the US Army. A voracious reader and a prolific writer, you can catch up with him on Facebook: Author_J_Walt_ Layne